MW01204272

# DANGEROUS GAME

T 84905
## By Jeri Massi

## PEABODY
### ADVENTURE SERIES

Bob Jones University Press, Greenville, South Carolina 29614

5/04

**A Dangerous Game**

Edited by Carolyn Cooper

Cover and illustrations by Del Thompson

© 1986 by Bob Jones University Press
Greenville, South Carolina 29614

ISBN 0-89084-347-3
Printed in the United States of America

20   19   18   17   16   15   14   13   12   11

Dedicated to
Marie Bayer
and
to the friends I made in San Francisco

# Contents

# Chapter One
# Martyrs and Other Relatives

You don't know about me if you haven't read Penny's book, called *Derwood, Inc.,* but that's okay. Don't run off and read it now. I can explain things anyway—a lot faster than she can. If you did read that book, you already know a lot about me—how I used to ambush Penny and her brother Jack all the time and try to rough them up.

You might say I was the neighborhood bully, and I was awfully fond of putting bricks through the windows of people I didn't like. Then after I met Mrs. Bennett and started taking care of her yard, I sort of quit a lot of my dirty tricks.

And then I became a Christian too, just like Jack and Penny Derwood—well, wait a second. Not *just* like Jack and Penny Derwood. I still get mad a lot and want to toss bricks through windows or go on rampages like I used to do. But I will say I've cut down on the rampages, though they aren't what you call *extinct* yet.

The people at church say it's a shame I'm a foster kid and had such a rough beginning, but I figure it wasn't too bad. Once you read this story, you'll probably agree that I was better fitted for this adventure than Jack and

Penny would have been. My only problem is that I'm not very smart—kind of dumb, if you want to know the truth. But it turned out—well, I'll tell it in order.

Anyway, I was over at Mrs. Bennett's one day, resting after I mowed her lawn. It had been hot outside, like the inside of a heated-up car engine, and she was making me lunch and filling me up with ice tea in the meanwhile. Sometimes to myself I pretended she was my real mother or that she was my foster mother, and I liked watching her.

She went on and on talking about a bunch of people called the martyrs. At first I thought they were something like the Italians or Hungarians, only I couldn't understand why every single one of them got killed or jailed. I've known lots of Italians, and none of them got killed, although once Antonio D'Ambrosio fell off the bleachers and broke his leg. He said a guy from a football team across town came up and pushed him to keep him from playing, but I think he just fell.

Anyway, she was going on and on about these martyrs, and I had just about decided they were probably related— maybe a bunch of cousins with lots of aunts and uncles, when she looked at me and said, "William,"—that's my real name, but other people call me Scruggs—"what would you do if a man threatened to hurt you unless you stopped going to church?"

I swallowed a gulp of tea and said, "I'd kick him in the shins if he was bigger than me, and then I'd find his house and shove a brick through his window. I'd show him if he tried to take me away from church, all right." And I meant that, too. Folks at church don't fight or yell or cuss like I'm used to hearing, and there's tons of little old ladies who make a fuss over me. Nobody's taking me away from church, I can tell you that. And I wouldn't care if he was bigger than me, either.

"Oh, William, can't you stop teasing?" she asked. "I want you to be serious!"

I looked up. I didn't understand why she was scolding. Mrs. Bennett never yells. She just kind of tells me I've done something wrong, and it hurts to hear it because I don't mean to. I'm just dumb.

"What'd I say wrong?" I asked. "I really would kick him. Nobody will take me away from church. I want to keep going!"

Then she softened up. "I know," she said quickly. "I didn't mean just not going to church. I wanted to know how you would feel if somebody tried to stop you from being a Christian."

"How could that happen? I am one. It's just the way it is."

"Well, I was talking about the martyrs," she told me.

"Those martyrs again," I said. "Who were they, anyway? Were you thinking they might be relatives of mine?"

Then her eyes got big. "You mean you don't understand what a martyr is?"

I finally decided it must have been something like an airplane pilot or tree surgeon—a profession. "Is it like a job?" I asked. But I felt my face burning because I got the idea that only dumb people don't know what martyrs are.

"No," she said gently. "Sit down, son. I'll explain it." She brought my sandwich to me and refilled my glass, and while I ate she told me more about the martyrs.

I'd never heard stuff like that—all about lions and gladiators, and men and women and even little kids not being afraid of anything. I wanted her to tell me about more of them, but she said, "Well, I have an old abridged version of *Foxe's Book of Martyrs* you can borrow."

"Does anybody get to be a martyr nowadays?" I asked.

"Yes, all the time."

"Even in Wisconsin?"

"Well, mostly in places like Russia and China, but in other countries, too."

"I don't think I could be a martyr," I said. "I don't feel very forgiving. I'd end up by beating somebody up."

"You have a while to grow yet. You're not even fourteen."

"I'm pretty grown up. I'm already in high school." That, by the way, is another curious thing. I used to do well in school before I quit trying. I did so well when I was a little kid that they boosted me up an extra grade. Don't ask me how a guy as dumb as me could do that well in school, because I'll tell you, I don't know.

After lunch I cleaned out the garage for her and hosed it down, and then I rested on the living room couch because it had been so hot outside. I only meant to cool off before I walked home, but next thing I knew, I was opening my eyes, and the sky outside the window was gray.

"I called your foster parents and told them you would eat dinner here," Mrs. Bennett said.

Mrs. Bennett eats in her dining room every night. It doesn't matter if she's the only one eating. She says it makes her feel more civilized to use the dining room for supper.

I watched her from the couch while she set out plates and forks and all. The dining room lamp put a nice glow on her gray hair, and she had an apron on. I think that when a guy's a foster kid and a Christian, too, he learns to hang on to pictures like that in his mind.

It used to be I would have made fun of Mrs. Bennett and thought she was just an old lady, but now I spent most of my devotions time praying I could be her foster kid someday. Like maybe some day she would just say, "Look, why bother the coming and going? Be my son, and it'll be more convenient that way." I hadn't ever told her that before, but I was pretty sure she had guessed it. I hoped she was giving it time, considering how it would work out. A guy can't push that sort of thing, but he can pray.

After we ate, I told her I would see her at church the next day, and then I left. It was very dark—daylight-saving time had only been going a couple weeks—but the streets in Peabody are safe. Not like Chicago, where I lived a couple years.

But as I was walking along from one streetlight to the next, I started getting this feeling—like somebody was behind me. Something about my own footsteps echoing too much to be mine. I kept turning around, but I couldn't see anybody. So I decided I'd better take a short cut and duck out of sight. I mean, I had plenty of people who still would have liked to get even with me for things I'd done before I got saved.

So I went through somebody's side yard and cut through along a hedge to the next street over. Then I waited and listened, and sure enough, somebody had been coming along after me, but he'd stopped when he'd heard me stop. I just caught the sound of his last footstep. I followed the hedge to the next street over and waited.

I was facing one side of a hedge of forsythia in bloom, and there was a yard to my back and the street along my left side. Whoever was following me, I figured, was on the same side of the hedge and could see me better than I could see him, what with the light from the streetlight shining down on me.

I was at his mercy there; best thing to do was run for it across the street and into another yard. I took off quick and made it.

I dived through another hedge, close to the bottom where there's some space between the branches, squiggled my way through several pounds of dirt along the roots, and then stomached my way behind a lilac bush. By this time I was in a maze of back yards and bushes. I watched in the direction I had come and didn't see anything moving.

That didn't make sense because I'd made plenty of noise getting through that last hedge. The guy following me would have at least figured the direction I'd gone. But I waited and waited, and nothing happened. I decided I'd sound him out, so I creeped backward on all fours, staying low and in the shadows, and when I got up alongside a house, I started barking. I can imitate dogs and cats good enough to fool people. It's one of my favorite tricks. Something a few yards off scurried away. But I didn't know who or what it was, and I wasn't sure it was gone. Maybe whoever was following me had just retreated at the sound of a dog.

I barked a bit and didn't hear anything; then I waited some more. I'd just started barking again when a window over my head opened and a woosh of freezing water over my shoulders took my breath away. "Be quiet out there!" a man's voice yelled. "Bad dog!"

I grabbed a rock out of the dirt and was going to get him back for that, I'll tell you, when I remembered how I'd been praying about my temper and how upset Mrs. Bennett had gotten the last time I'd busted a guy's window. I held my breath, squeezed my eyes shut, and told myself there wasn't any point in getting mad. For once the rage went out of me, and I was okay.

Then I dropped back down and crawled away, fast. I stayed in the yards because I didn't want to show up on the street with my shirt and hair soaking wet. All the way home I ran my fingers through my hair to try to comb it down, and I wrung out my shirt. As I walked up to the house where I lived, I saw a little white paper stuck on the front door.

I glanced at it, and in the glow of the light from the window, I read the words:

*BEWARE THE JUGGLER!*

## Chapter Two
# The Send-up

I can't explain how I knew that that paper was meant for me. I just knew that it was. Besides, Mom and Dad Wilson—my foster parents—are not the sort of people who get mysterious notes. I'm the biggest adventure they ever had in their lives.

I think when they took me as a foster kid, they were expecting somebody like Tom Sawyer. I wasn't much of a replacement. Dad Wilson did teach me to raise bait, and it's kind of fun because I like bugs and worms, but I hate sitting by a creek for hours while I itch and twitch, waiting for some fish to fall for it and get the bait. Fishermen always say it's the thrill of the challenge—you know, being smart enough to bag a big one. The way I see it, it's pretty sad for a guy to think it's a big deal to outwit a fish.

But I did go fishing with Dad Wilson, especially after I became a Christian, because Mom and Dad Wilson aren't saved. I tried to be especially good so that they'd notice it and listen when I talked to them about God. But it didn't work too well because I still lost my temper sometimes, and every time I lost my temper, I could see that they were figuring I hadn't changed at all.

I used to be *really* bad, which was why I'd been moved through so many foster homes so fast. Mom and Dad Wilson had stood me longer than most could—about three years, and then I'd gotten saved. Right away I'd quit hanging around on the street with my friends, and I'd quit the other things I used to do, like stealing from the stores and all that. But whenever I got mad, I always wanted to bust a window. I just couldn't seem to beat that one habit.

Anyway, they let me go to church and do things with the church kids, but they weren't very convinced yet that I'd changed. I wondered if I should tell them about that note—*Beware The Juggler!* Seemed like if I did, they would just worry and maybe think I'd been up to something sneaky. And it seemed to be my business. But then again it was on *their* door, so maybe they deserved to know. And besides, I was trying to be like a real son now. It seemed like a guy would tell his parents that sort of thing.

I worried about it while I showered and got my robe on, and I tucked the paper into my Bible and kept thinking about it while I was trying to read. Then after I was in bed I kept thinking about it, and I finally decided I would ask Mrs. Bennett at church and do whatever she thought was best.

The next day was clear and hot, and my shirt stuck to me through the whole ride on the church bus. And my tie felt too tight. The way I like to wear a tie doesn't look right—all loose and comfortable. I see pictures of these handsome guys in newspapers and magazines wearing their ties down like that, and they look cool and ready for action, but when I wear it that way, I look like a slob. So I keep it pulled up tight to my collar, and the collar buttoned, and then I swelter and wish that somebody would invent an elegant T-shirt and give us guys a break.

I meant to ask Mrs. Bennett about the note, but when I met her after Sunday school, she looked different somehow, like maybe something was wrong, and I didn't know what to say. I never thought about things going wrong for her. They go wrong for me all the time, but she always seemed to be on top of things.

But she didn't say anything different, only looked at me a little longer than usual it seemed, and then led me to our seats.

"Has your caseworker been over this weekend?" she asked.

"No, not until next weekend, I think," I told her. Then she did look troubled, and I would have asked her why, but it was time to sing a hymn and start the service. I forgot about the note with worrying about what was eating her. It put me in a sweat to have her wondering about my caseworker and all that. I wondered if I was in trouble— if I'd done something wrong or if maybe the Children's Aid group was going to give me a once-over for some reason.

Back when I'd been bad, I'd come close a couple times to going to what's called a group home. That's a place where they put the kids who act like jailbirds. It's not a reform school, but for some it's the last step before reform school. I'd never cared before, but now I worried. Maybe somebody had reviewed my folder and thought I should be sent off somewhere—before I could prove I'd changed. I didn't want to get sent away.

She noticed I was in a sweat about wondering why she asked about my caseworker, and during the offering she patted my hand. That's another thing about Mrs. Bennett, she always wears gloves and a hat to church. Not many women wear hats, and nobody wears gloves, but she always wears both. She says it's proper. The hat I can understand, but I don't know where the idea of gloves comes from.

"It's all right," she whispered. "You aren't in trouble. Settle down."

"Okay." I felt better. We sang another hymn and then listened to the sermon. Afterward in the crowd of people we couldn't talk to each other. Everybody at church is friendly, always shaking your hand and asking how you are, and I've always got half the deacons inviting me over for dinner or Ping-Pong or hiring me to cut their grass. I think I remind everybody of an orphan, and they all want to help me.

Out at the church bus I told Mrs. Bennett good-bye and I would see her at the evening service, and she surprised me by kissing my cheek and saying, "I'll see you tonight or this afternoon, if you want to come over, son." And then she was gone, and all the little kids were milling around me so that I couldn't run after her. I don't know why I wanted to run after her, except that nobody ever kisses *me*. I don't matter very much to people.

Then I hoisted myself onto the bus and waited to get home and out of those duds.

But when I got home, the caseworker's car was in the driveway. If you haven't figured it out, a caseworker is a social worker who watches out for a certain number of foster kids and keeps up with how they're doing. Caseworkers bring both bad news and good.

I hopped off the bus and went inside, loosening my tie. I didn't care if I looked like a slob because it was choking me even worse now that I knew the caseworker had come.

"There he is!" Miss Stevens said pleasantly when I came in. "I have a surprise for you, Bill."

It didn't sound like I was in trouble. My heart stopped pounding. "What's up?" I asked weakly. Mom and Dad Wilson were looking at me with smiles that seemed glued on.

"A very wealthy aunt of yours has been granted permanent guardianship of you."

"I didn't know I had an aunt," I said.

"Neither did we, but her claim checks out, and she's a *very* pleasant woman. She means to put you in a private school and travel with you in a few years. Oh, she's wonderful—owns a stable of horses and keeps dogs. You'll love her."

"Couldn't I stay here?" I asked.

Miss Stevens looked uncomfortable under her top crust of delight and happiness. "I'm sorry, Bill. She's been granted your permanent guardianship. She is, after all, your aunt."

"Okay."

"You'll be moving out there in two weeks."

"*Out there?*" I asked. "Where is *out there?*"

Miss Stevens's smile wavered. "San Francisco. Won't that be fun?"

## Chapter Three
# Certain Mental Preparations

Nobody's proud of crying, so I won't tell you about that part, but when it was over, Mrs. Bennett made me take off my jacket and tie and sat me down, and she brought me ice tea, and told me to drink it slowly. Then she called Mom and Dad Wilson and told them I was okay, I had just run over to her house to tell her I was going to San Francisco. I had left Mom and Dad pretty calmly but quickly because I didn't want anybody to see me that upset, and I thought by the time I got to Mrs. Bennett's, I would be okay. But as soon as I saw her, I got worse.

"I'll write to you, William. I'm a very good letter-writer," she said softly. "And there are good churches out there. The people will be just as friendly as here in Peabody. Jack and Penny Derwood have visited out there, and they liked it there. They've told me so."

"You knew I was going, didn't you?" I asked.

"Yes, I knew."

"Why didn't you tell me?" I asked her.

"For a reason you may not understand, William. It wasn't my place to tell you."

"If it wasn't your place to tell me, why did the Agency talk to you before they talked to me?" I asked.

She hesitated, looked down, and then looked at me. "Because the Wilsons and I had agreed that it would have been best for me to take you—" My heart jumped at the words. I half-stood up. Her next words crushed me. "But the Agency thought otherwise. Your aunt will take you. I was surprised they gave her your permanent guardianship so quickly, but they did." I sank back into the chair.

"Even if I asked to live with you—" I began, but she was shaking her head.

"It's done," she said.

So I sat there fiddling with my glass, and at last I said, "Why did God bring us so close to it and then ruin it?"

"The story isn't over yet," she told me. "When it is, you'll see that your prayers were answered—perhaps not as you expected, but He did hear you."

"Is it because I'm so bad?" I asked her. "Is God mad at me?"

She shook her head. "No. When He sees you, He sees that you're redeemed. God may chastise you in love, but He won't punish you in wrath. You're saved from His wrath." She refilled my glass. "Besides, nobody is good enough to *deserve* a blessing from God. Every blessing comes from grace."

But it still rankled—to be so close! I felt like breaking a window—my aunt's, wherever she was. But I tried to squelch the thought. Seemed wrong to be thinking about breaking a window when Mrs. Bennett was talking about the Lord.

That night at church, Jack Derwood came and sat next to me at the youth group meeting.

"Heard you're moving," he said. Jack and his sister Penny used to be two of the main kids I picked on. At first when I'd started coming to church, they'd thought I was trying to fool everybody, but since winter we'd been trying to be friends or at least not be enemies. Penny's almost my age, and Jack's a year younger, but they both always seemed younger to me, probably because I was a year ahead of Penny in school, taller, and acted like a teenager before I was one.

"Yeah, I'm going to San Francisco."

"We got an uncle out there—Uncle Bill. Birky is his last name. Maybe we'll see you out there. He's always asking us to come out."

"Really?" I didn't even try to sound enthusiastic. That's Jack's life story. Everybody likes him—everybody except that gal smuggler that crossed tracks with him and his sister. Jack and Penny botched up her whole operation and broke up the smuggling ring. Then to top it, they rescued some scientist's kid who'd been kidnaped by her and her gang. But other than crooks, everybody likes Jack. He makes friends with people on the spot.

"Have you been out there yet?" I asked him.

"Yeah, after we left our Aunt Irene's last summer, we got in touch with our uncle, and he invited us out over Christmas, so we went. He lives in a place called Mountain View, just outside the city. He said he wanted us back over the summer, so maybe we'll be out to see you in a few weeks—soon as school gets out."

"What makes you think he'll ask you right away?" I asked.

"Oh, Uncle Bill's great. He had a terrific time with us and keeps talking about us coming back to see him. I'm sure he'll want us back as soon as possible. We're his oldest niece and nephew, and he likes showing us around. Hey, Penny, come over here!" he called to his sister.

Some kids get all the luck. Jack Derwood isn't dumb like me; he's going to be handsome, and he's got rich relatives all over the place just begging him and his sister to come visit.

Penny came over and sat down. The youth meeting started, and I was glad.

My mind wasn't on it. I slid my hands into the cool leaves of my Bible, the room being hot in the church basement, and my fingers touched that slip of paper I had tucked away and forgotten about. I pulled it out and glanced at it. *Beware The Juggler!* I wondered who The Juggler was. Nobody in Peabody juggled for a living. Had to be a code name or nickname. Maybe Jack would have an idea. That smuggler lady he and Penny had tangled with had sported some crazy code name—Rumplestiltskin or Tom Thumb or something like that.

"Hey," I said when the youth meeting ended. "Look at this, Jack. I found it on my door last night."

Jack glanced at it, and Penny looked over his shoulder.

"Somebody was following me on the way home," I explained. "I got away and hid, but when I came home, this was on the door."

We started up to the auditorium for the evening service. "Maybe it's a code name," Jack suggested. "But why would anybody drag *you* into something like that? You've never been involved with crooks, have you?"

"Of course not!" I exclaimed, sore at his remark. Sometimes I get tired of people thinking I'm some kind of jailbird.

"Has your family, maybe?" Jack asked.

"How should I know? I'm a foster kid! Gimme the paper; you're no help!" I jammed the paper into my pocket and would have stamped away. Don't ask me why, but

I never think about being a foster kid until I get around church kids. Then I get really edgy about it.

"Wait, Scruggs," Jack called. "I'm sorry. I didn't mean to insult you."

"Jack says dumb things all the time," Penny added. "He doesn't mean them. Come on and sit with us."

The last thing I wanted to do was sit with the all-American family, but Penny added, "Just us three. Come on." So I did. It's hard to stay mad at two kids who want to be friends. By the time we got seated, the service was starting.

Jack leaned over and whispered, "Just wait until you fly over the Rockies. It'll take your breath away."

It took my breath away all right when he said that. I just realized I would have to fly out there. *Fly!* My spine went rigid and my eyes went glassy. *Fly!*

I suddenly realized I had a fear of flying.

## Chapter Four
# A Fear of Flying

Mrs. Bennett drove me to the airport. The hot spell had at last broken, and it was a usual spring day, except for how miserable I felt. I don't think I'd ever felt so miserable.

"Do you know who Mr. Blackthorn is?" she asked as we pulled onto the interstate for the long drive to the airport.

"No. Does he go to our church?" I asked.

"Oh, no. His house is behind my house and about two blocks over."

"Oh."

Then we were both quiet. At last I couldn't take it any more. "Okay," I said. "I did it. I broke his window last night. My last fling."

The thing with Mrs. Bennett is that she doesn't get mad. Nothing makes her mad. You could tap dance on her kitchen table, and she wouldn't get mad. She looked at me and said softly, "I'm disappointed in you."

And it hurt in my chest when she said that. I felt my face burn deep red. In looking back it seemed babyish to have done it—just to have up and flung the rock into the pane of glass and to feel so satisfied to hear the jangle when it broke. It always seemed babyish once I'd done it.

"Were you out wandering the streets last night?" she asked.

I didn't look at her. "Yes."

"William, I told you to come to my house instead of doing that," she said. "You always get in trouble if you wander idle on the streets."

"I felt like fighting last night," I told her sulkily. "I figured I'd meet up with somebody sooner or later who had a grudge against me."

She sighed and looked tired and beaten. I hadn't done anything right in the last two weeks. Trouble, trouble, trouble—bad grades, big arguments. I'd quit reading my Bible because it was God's fault for making me move, and those rages of mine had gotten worse and worse.

"William, it's a long, hard fight when you fight God," she said at last. "It isn't anything a mother wants to see her son doing."

Then she didn't say anything else, and through most of the long ride we were silent, until I asked her if she would still miss me, and she told me she would.

"I'll write to that Blackthorn guy," I told her. "I'll tell him I did it, and I'll send him the money for it, once I earn enough. I'll tell him I'm sorry."

She looked at me, trying to be pleased even for that step, but I knew she was wishing I hadn't done it at all.

After that we talked more easily until we got to the airport. She led me to the baggage check and then took me to get my boarding pass. I could see big planes taxiing on the runway. The whole wall of the airport terminal was reinforced glass, so a person had the pleasure—or the agony—of watching the planes take off.

"Flight 323 to San Francisco, Gate 4, will begin boarding," a man said over a microphone. "First-class passengers and passengers with children may now board."

I felt sick.

A few minutes later, the voice over the microphone continued, "We will begin boarding from the rear of the plane. Rows twenty to thirty may now board."

I was in row eighteen. They would call me next. Suddenly my middle hurt, and I looked wildly around, and then back to Mrs. Bennett. It wasn't just being scared of flying; it was leaving, too.

"William, I'll invite you up over Thanksgiving or Christmas," she said. "I won't lose touch with you. Don't be afraid." And she kissed my cheek. I just stood there like a big lump—too dumb to say anything, I guess.

"Rows ten to thirty may now board," the voice said.

"I'll start reading my Bible again," I said, and I felt a burning creep up my face. I blush all the time. I don't know why. Then I tried to walk away, but I couldn't help asking, "You gonna pray that the Agency will change its mind?"

"William, God has promised me that you are a gift from Him to me," she said. "Don't be afraid." Then she kissed my other cheek. "You'd better board, my son."

"But how can you know something like that?" I asked. "How did God tell you that?"

"He tells things to the people who want His friendship," she said. "I'll pray for you. When you're God's friend, you'll understand better. Go on, son. Don't be afraid that you won't see me again. I know that you will."

And somehow I found myself walking with the others and looking back at her, and then I was in the middle of a crowd of the most bored people I've ever seen. They were bored before we even started.

We nudged and pushed past each other. Men grumbled and unfolded papers, and then made room for other people sliding into their seats in the narrow 727. Women with overstuffed shopping bags stood on tiptoe, cramming them into the compartments above their seats.

I sank into an aisle seat next to an older couple, but I didn't notice them much for trying to figure out how somebody could know something like that. And then I just felt blissful that she'd called me her son. And that she'd been sure we would see each other again. For a long, happy minute I thought of that and felt so much better that if I'd had a whole pile of rocks and a row of windows I wouldn't have been tempted to bust one of them.

I was just deciding that she was right—it was time to quit fighting God and start praying and reading my Bible again—when the plane started to taxi. My heart went into my mouth, and my prayer life was instantly renewed.

Okay, okay, so I shut my eyes when we took off. I mean, I read stories all the time about marines and soldiers who faint when they get medical shots. Now if they can faint over a needle, I can shut my eyes while taking off.

And maybe I did grab that old lady's hand, but maybe she grabbed mine. I don't know. I can't remember. I think I fainted.

Anyway, when I opened my eyes, the older man in the window seat was leaning against the window and steadying a 35-mm camera.

"Just beautiful, Edna," he was saying. "Just beautiful." That was when I realized I was holding onto her hand, and I let go and turned red. She smiled a sweet grandmotherly smile up at me and turned back to him.

"Oh, get one of the—uh—the things over there. What are they, anyway?" she asked him, pointing.

"Can't rightly tell from way up here," he said. "But I'll get a picture, dear. Get another roll ready, Nurse."

She chuckled and reached into his suit pocket for another roll of the film while he clicked away. The plane was circling. Now my stomach came up in my mouth along with my heart, but at least I couldn't see the ground with those two pressed against the window.

Quicker than you could think possible, they changed rolls of film. "Oh, here come the clouds. We're still ascending," she said. I looked forward and with a jolt saw that the plane was tilted upward. It made me sick to think about it. I gasped and shut my eyes.

"Poor boy looks sick," she said. "Albert, give him an antacid tablet."

"Right here, right here," he chuckled, reaching into his blue suitcoat and handing out antacid tablets to us both. He had on a matching sky-blue hat with a black band to go with his blue suitcoat, blue trousers, and pale blue shirt. Somehow he looked elegant all dressed up like that.

"That will make you feel better," she promised while I sucked on the tablet. But the plane turned again, and I almost choked.

"Why, it's not a sick stomach at all. Nor homesickness. The poor boy's afraid to fly!" she said. Everybody in the next row up turned around and looked at me, except the men with their newspapers. They went right on reading them and rattling them.

"I used to be scared too," the lady ahead of me said. "And this one time, coming into Seattle, the landing gear wouldn't lock into place. Anyway, it wouldn't register as locked. That was tense—let me tell you—"

"Oh that's nothing," a lady ahead of her said. "We were taxiing for take-off one time, and the right wing just shuddered and collapsed—terrible."

"Well, did you hear about that time the plane took off, and its whole baggage compartment fell out? All that luggage lost—"

"Oh, and wind shear, have you heard the latest on that?"

I pulled my juggling book out of my back pocket and started reading furiously. I'm not smart enough to be much of a reader, but anything was better than listening to half the plane's passengers telling horror stories of plane crashes.

I had started reading up on juggling, trying to figure out that message, and I had a how-to book on it. It was pretty heavy going, but I wanted to make sure I didn't miss any hidden messages that a juggler would understand.

I figured there was some chance that whoever left me that note knew I was going to San Francisco. Maybe I wouldn't meet that juggler guy until I got there.

Just then there was this flash. I jerked my head up, stunned—like maybe we were crashing or something. But it was just Albert or whatever his name was, taking my picture.

"Oh, dear me," his wife said, "We just love keeping track of who we meet and what they do. Smile now, and I'll move closer."

She leaned her head next to mine, and her husband clicked the camera again. "Perfect!" he exclaimed.

"You two fly all the time?" I asked.

"Oh, not very much," she told me. "Every Christmas we go somewhere, and just now we're flying out for a little vacation. That's all. Where are you from?"

"Peabody, Wisconsin," I told her.

"Oh dear. Peabody. Do you know where that is, Honey?" she asked him.

"Let's see now." He fished around in his suitcoat pocket and pulled out a pocket atlas. Licking one thumb, he flipped through it until he came to the page he wanted.

"Oh, Peabody. Small town, eh? But it's listed—got one library, looks like, and a hospital."

"We used to travel by car quite a bit," she explained. "Until we found out how much fun planes are. Oh me, if we could just start over, I know we would both be pilots."

"If I could start over, I'd be on a train," I grumbled.

"Oh dear, there's nothing to be afraid of. Flying is very safe."

Just then the plane lurched and seemed to take a dip. I grabbed the arms of the seat.

"Just turbulence. Just turbulence," she said. "Albert, where's that little pamphlet that explains these things?"

"Got it right here," he said, fishing around in his pockets and pulling out a little tract.

I tried to read it, but I felt sick. After a while I handed it back and looked at my juggling book. Juggling seemed simple enough, from the looks of the book. Plenty of diagrams to explain it.

"Oh say, I could teach you juggling faster than that," a voice said.

I looked up. I was about ready to tell whoever was snooping over my shoulder to mind his own business and leave me alone, but then I saw the guy wasn't bragging. I could see it in his face. He was bent over a little and smiling with a nice, easy smile, like I reminded him of his little brother or something. He was thin like a track runner, mustached, with short brown hair that had gray streaks in it. I figured he was graying early because he looked pretty athletic and young otherwise.

"Come on up to my seat," he told me. "I've got some stuff in my luggage."

So I followed him up the aisle into first class, where the seats are bigger. None of the attendants seemed to mind.

The guy sat me down across the row. "Honey, this is—" he began, then looked at me. "Say, what's your name?"

"Scruggs."

He tilted his head, like he thought it was a nutty name, but then he said, "I'm Tom Blancke, and this is Jeannie, my wife." He turned to her. "Where's your eye make-up? That will do perfectly," he said.

She was small, with long straight hair and pretty eyes. "In my handbag," she said with a sigh and let him rummage around in her purse until he came up with three little round bottles all about the same size. She must have been used to his juggling with her make-up.

"This is great," he said. "Now watch. To start, just throw one of these little bottles from hand to hand. But you have to make a nice, smart arc up in the air. Let the bottle come up to about your nose or eye level, and then down smoothly into your other hand. Don't reach up to catch it. Just let it take its time."

That was easy. I did it a while as some of the passengers stuck their heads around to watch.

"Terrific. Now take two—one in each hand—and imagine there's a hoop attached to your nose. Arc both of them up to go through that hoop and land in the opposite hands."

I tried, but they smacked into each other in the air.

"Let the one from the right hand lead a little bit," he told me. "You've got terrific aim. The arc of your throw is perfect. I can see you understand the principle of juggling."

Maybe it was silly, but I felt good when he said that. Especially when he said it in front of the other people, and they smiled. I guess I've always been dumb. Maybe I'd been born to juggle and never known it.

I tried it again, and I had to reach out to catch one of the bottles, but each time I tried it, I got better. After a few minutes, he said, "Now it's simple, Scruggs. When you juggle with two hands, you're only ever keeping two of the objects up at the same time. You just have to keep your rhythm calm and slow, and relax with it." Then he did it, and suddenly I could see how a juggler does it. He just keeps throwing things one at a time in the perfect arc, aiming for the pretend hoop on the end of his nose, and if he does it in a steady rhythm, he can keep three objects going. Two are always either coming or going in the air, while one is being caught and thrown.

At first I was too nervous, because everybody in first class was watching, even the attendants. But then when they got bored—I kept goofing up—they turned back around, and pretty soon I got it when no one was looking. I was juggling.

Then they turned around again to watch, but I didn't notice. I didn't care. I was glad a dumb guy like me could do that. There was a flash.

"Got it, Edna!" and I knew that the guy and his wife from my seat had come up to watch. They pulled back the curtain from the rest of the plane, and some of the people looked up and clapped.

But after everybody left us alone again, the man taught me to juggle two with one hand, which is harder than three objects with two hands. But once I could do two with one hand, I could do two with each hand, and that made four. The guy found a little ball of yarn in his wife's sewing bag, and we used that.

He taught me all sorts of tricks with juggling, and then he asked where I was going.

"San Francisco. To live with my aunt."

"In the city?" he asked.

"No, a place called Palo Alto." That was what Miss Stevens had told me. It sounded like a crazy name to me. Tom told me most people said it meant the White Heights.

"Jeannie and I live in Stanford," he told me. "Look us up if you need anything."

I went back to my seat. Only forty-five minutes to go. I got the nerve to introduce myself to the older couple, and they told me they were Mr. and Mrs. McCune. Then I told them all about juggling and how easy it was.

"It can't be that easy!" she told me. "You have a gift for it."

"No, that's crazy. I don't have gifts like that. It's just easy."

"My, my," Mr. McCune said, pushing back his blue hat. "That fellow up in first class is quite a juggler himself to have taught you so fast."

Then for a second I didn't hear anything else. A juggler. Was that who I was supposed to watch out for? Maybe that Tom guy was an embezzler or one of those crooks who gyp money out of little old ladies like my aunt. And somebody had warned me. He was already trying to worm his way in with me.

# Chapter Five
# Aunt Caroline

I stayed back with the McCunes. One minute we were flying along, and then suddenly it seemed like a knife got wedged between my ears and I couldn't hear for a second.

"What was that?" I asked when it stopped.

"We've started our descent," Mrs. McCune told me. "You have sensitive ears. So have I. The change in pressure bothers me, too."

"We're dropping?" I yelled. Everybody turned around and looked at me. Except the businessmen. They were asleep.

"Shhh. Yes," she said in a low voice. "Don't be afraid."

"I'm not afraid. I'm terrified. I don't wanna watch." And I shut my eyes.

"Oh, but it's beautiful," she said.

"Got it, Edna! Lake Tahoe!" And I heard the camera clicking busily at the window.

It did go fast. "Just look this once," she pleaded. I opened my eyes and saw a wide, green sea under us.

"The ocean!" I exclaimed.

"No, it's just the bay. The Golden Gate Bridge is out there."

It was beautiful. Even a dunce like me could see that. And it was hard to be scared because it was so flat. The runway came right up to the bay. One second we were over water, and the next second I saw asphalt under the wings. Then suddenly I felt the speed of the plane as we touched the ground. There was a terrific rushing sound.

"Reverse thrust!" Mr. McCune called over the noise. It was the one part of the flight I really liked. Everybody else looked bored. I decided I was glad I had sat next to the McCunes. At least they were never bored. They liked everything—even me, as it turned out.

"I still think you're a clever boy," Mrs. McCune said. "You keep up that juggling, and someday we might see you at Giarhdelli Square."

"Where?" I asked.

"Never mind. You'll find out for yourself. It's a lovely place. All sorts of jugglers perform there."

I hadn't brought any carry-on luggage, so I left them while they got their things, and I worked my way up the crowded aisle. And what do you know, but there was Tom the Juggler and his wife.

"Do you need a ride anywhere?" he asked me.

"No," I told him and didn't add anything. I decided I didn't trust him. He just looked at me like maybe I was crazy to be rude.

"Anybody meeting you?" he asked.

"My aunt," I said. "I'll see you later." And I pushed by him.

I went up the walkway and out into the crowded gate room. "There you are, Scruggs!" A short, round guy with hair on the sides of his head wrung me by the hands.

"Don't know me, eh?" he boomed. "Well, well, that's all right. You will, you will! I recognized you from Jack and Penny's description. I'm their Uncle Bill. You call me Uncle Bill, too, eh? Welcome to San Francisco."

"Nice to meet you," I told him, hoping it was polite enough to a guy who's a lawyer and respectable. "Who did you come out to meet?"

"Why, I came to meet you, boy!" he boomed. "Jack and Penny wrote, said you were new out here, and didn't know anybody. I want you to call on me if you need anything."

Just then two things happened at once. A small woman in her forties or maybe fifties suddenly appeared from behind a knot of people. And Tom and Jeannie came up behind me from the walkway. Mr. Birky had stopped me so that I was sort of in everybody's way.

"William!" the woman said. She eyed Mr. Birky like he was crazy for coming up and shaking my hand. She stepped forward and pretty nearly elbowed him out of the way. "I'm your Aunt Caroline, William. It's time to go home."

"Oh, so you're his Aunt Caroline!" Mr. Birky boomed. "Pleased, so pleased to meet you!" And he wrung her hand, too. From behind me, Tom said, "That's your aunt, Scruggs?"

I looked back, annoyed. I figured that here was where this crook tried to sell her the Golden Gate Bridge or something like that.

"Yeah," I snarled.

Then my aunt got a look at Tom. For one tiny second, I thought she recognized him, but then maybe I was wrong. She looked at me. "It's time to go, William." For all her frailness, she seemed pretty strong-willed.

But Tom stepped between us. I was ready to jump on him or fight him or do anything. By now I was sure he was The Juggler.

But all he said was, "Oh! You must be Scruggs' . . . aunt." He added that last word like it was something he didn't believe or something he thought she should be ashamed of. But he held out his hand to her, and she shook it.

"Yes," she said. "The poor boy must be tired. It's time for us to go."

Suddenly Mr. Birky threw his arm around me. "Say, boy, I want you to feel at home with me, all right? I'll pick you up for church on Sunday. Here's my card. It's got my home phone number on it."

"Thanks, Mr. Birky." I took his card.

"And look here, you call me Uncle Bill."

"Okay."

"I'd ask you to lunch, but your aunt's in an all-fired hurry to get you home. Well, maybe she's right. See you on Sunday." Then he shook my hand again and walked off. I don't know. A guy like me doesn't have much sense, but somehow I felt less comfortable after he left, like some kind of protection had left with him.

"Scruggs." That was Tom again. He was pulling out a card, too. "If you need anything, here's my card, too." And he put his big hand on my shoulder and looked serious and kind of unhappy. "You sure you won't be going back home, soon?"

"He *is* home!" My aunt cut in. But Tom looked at her again, and it seemed like they knew each other—or at least like they didn't like each other right off the bat.

"Well then, call me," he said, "if you need *anything*."

"Come along, William," my aunt said.

"Good-bye," Tom told me. His wife Jeannie looked as puzzled as I felt. But I decided that there couldn't be anything wrong with Tom, even if he was The Juggler I was supposed to watch out for.

Aunt Caroline was small and slender and must have been beautiful once. She was wrapped up in sweaters and shawls because her circulation was bad, she said, and she stooped a little when she walked. But her face wasn't wrinkled, only tired-looking with middle age. Her hair looked soft, and there was plenty of it—mostly gray but shot with rich brown streaks.

She took me out to a limousine—a real one with a chauffeur and everything. My heart did a double flop. Everybody back home had told me she was rich, but I hadn't thought about it at all until that minute. The chauffeur ushered us into the back, climbed into the front, and pulled the car out smoother than that plane had felt.

"This is great!" I said, and I watched the interstate through the tinted windows. "I've never even been in a Cadillac or nothing, and this beats them by a mile! Did you have it custom made?"

"Oh, a customer has plenty of choices when he buys a limo," she said sweetly. "I didn't ask for anything that they weren't ready to put into it. I'm glad you like it."

"I like animals, too," I told her, turning around. "Do you have horses?"

"Yes, but not in Palo Alto. They're in my estate in the Big Valley."

I looked back at the interstate. We were sweeping past buildings like I'd never seen before—stuccoed buildings of pale pink or gold. And there were palm trees, too. I could see them here and there in tall clumps.

"It's like being in Mexico—that's what the houses look like," I said.

She laughed. "I had heard you were worldly wise, but you're just a babe in arms, my boy," she told me. "This is simply Californian decor—a mixture of Spanish, Mexican, and western." Then she laughed again, and I looked at her, uncomfortable. She was laughing at me for being dumb.

"Oh dear, don't blush," she said. "I wouldn't have thought it of you."

"What do you think of me?" I blurted. "You must have heard plenty."

"I did indeed, but so long as you obey me, we should get along fine."

"I'll obey you," I told her. "I'm not like I was before. You'll see that." And I turned to look out the window again and prayed really hard that I would never break another window again, no matter how mad I got.

"Then we should get along well," she said. "Neither of us will have anything to worry about."

# Chapter Six
# The Plot Thickens

After about forty-five minutes, the sleek limo slid down an exit ramp. Around us, cars zoomed back and forth, almost heedless of each other, but there were no accidents.

"Yes," she said, noticing what I was thinking, "they do drive fast around here. Not like where you're from, I'm sure. But they're accurate, and they obey stop signs. I find myself more comfortable in California traffic than in any other traffic, especially New Jersey."

I had the feeling of being closely watched by my aunt, but I guessed it was normal for her to watch me, with my reputation. I turned back to the tinted window. We were gliding along smooth roads of a residential section. The houses that bordered the road were big—some of them hidden by impressive brick or stone walls. It was certainly a ritzy neighborhood.

The chauffeur's name was Rick, and he took my bags in, giving me a smirk when I offered to get them. I didn't like him; that was a fact. We'd pulled into a long, low building. It looked like the Alamo to me, but I didn't make any comments about its design. It had a wide yard, a swimming pool, and a tool shed out in the back yard, and it was surrounded by a high stucco wall for privacy.

Inside was cool and dim. Hallways stretched everywhere. It was a house of a good size. "The maid's apartment is that way," she said, nodding down one hallway. "Rick sleeps in the old servant's quarters along the side of the house. Your room is this way." With Rick and the luggage following, my aunt showed me down a long hallway and into a room divided into two halves. One half had a double bed, a chest of drawers, a mirror, and a closet. It was separated from the other half by what I took to be a partition. But when we came around the partition, I saw that it was a huge bookcase on the other side, already loaded with books, and this half of the room was a study with a desk, an armchair, and a reading lamp. It would be nice, I thought, for devotions and practicing my juggling, but otherwise I wasn't much on studying.

"Nice, isn't it, nephew?" she asked me, admiring it herself.

"Pretty nice," I agreed, but I felt a pang for the worn-out and comfortable furniture at Mrs. Bennett's. Something told me that a guy couldn't go out and mow the grass for Aunt Caroline and then be rewarded with lots of smiles and glasses of ice tea. She could just as easily hire somebody to do that kind of thing.

My aunt turned and looked me full in the face. I realized that she had very young and merry eyes, which took me by surprise when I considered how she walked so old and tired.

"I hope that you'll like it here, Scruggs," she said. "I hope that we become friends."

"Sure," I said.

"And you'll find how pleasant it is to be rich. Isn't it pleasant, Rick?" she asked the chauffeur.

"Very, Miss Grady," he said.

"I'll have to try it yet and see," I told her.

"Good. Dinner is in three hours. You may want to rest between now and then. Come, Rick."

And she walked out with him. I came back around to make sure they'd left. "Being rich isn't as nice as being in Peabody," I mumbled and threw myself onto the bed. I jammed my face into my pillows and threw my mind back to Peabody, Wisconsin.

I didn't expect to sleep, but traveling by plane had worn me out more than I'd figured. The sky was a pale purple-blue outside the window, and the room was cool when I woke up. Someone was knocking on my door.

"It's the maid, sir," a voice called. "Are you awake yet?"

I jumped up and opened the door. "Yeah, I'm up."

She was a pretty girl and seemed very young, scarcely past her teens. But maybe that's what teenagers did for work in Palo Alto: waited on rich people. She smiled. "Miss Grady has gone out for the evening, but she wanted to be sure you had your dinner. It's out in the dining room."

"Here I come." I wondered where she had gone but was just as glad to eat alone.

The maid's name was Janet. She wore a pale blue dress and apron, but it didn't look like one of those frilly maid's uniforms like they wear in palaces. I found out that my aunt had a cook, too. When I went into the dining room, my place was set, and Janet told me what the cook had made me—Chicken Kiev it was called, with an appetizer of oysters on the half shell and some fancy mishmash of vegetables. I wouldn't have touched those oysters, except I didn't want to get the cook mad. I've heard about those cooks and how they rip their hair out and cry if you don't like their food. But I was definitely going to drop a hint for hamburgers or chili, maybe.

Janet waited on me while I ate, and I felt funny.

"Go on, take the night off," I told her. "I've been eatin' on my own since I was a kid. I can find my way around."

She laughed at me. "Oh no, sir. Miss Grady wants you to enjoy yourself, and you have to learn to be waited on. That's part of the game in California."

So I let her stand around and fuss. The chicken was pretty good, and she gave me coffee with real cream.

"Dessert?" she asked. I had to say no. Too much chicken. Then she offered to play checkers with me, so we did. I realized it was her duty to entertain me, and even though I liked her company, I felt like she was baby-sitting, so after two games I told her I would go to my room.

I was glad to be alone again. I unpacked and then rummaged around for my socks. Mom Wilson folds socks into little balls some way. They were perfect for juggling. I stood in front of the mirror in my room and practiced. After a while it got so easy that I looked at myself doing it, and I worked on looking easy and cheerful, like it was nothing. Then I'd look at the socks again, going up and down in their smooth arcs, then concentrate on my image in the mirror and how I was coming across. Scruggs Grady—the life of any party, I told myself. One guy who really knows how to play the game in California and act like being the only nephew of a rich aunt is terrific.

I got a fourth sock and worked on the double two-hand juggling, which was much harder. I missed every now and then, so I went back to the three-object juggling.

Then I looked at myself in the mirror, and I could see the lamp behind me and the window. In the window, half of a man's face was peering in at me.

## Chapter Seven
# Who Are the Bad Guys?

It disappeared as soon as I laid eyes on it, but I shouted and flung open the window. This window looked onto the back yard, where the pool and tool shed were. I climbed through and ran across the grass. Just ahead of me, I could make out a man's shape running for the wall. But the yard was almost pitch dark as we got farther from my window. There were no stars or moon for light.

There must have been a bench on the lawn that he didn't see. I heard him crack his shins against something and go over, so without checking myself, I gave a leap and came down on both cement and flesh. Somehow we were tangled up with a cement bench that he had tripped over and upset.

I didn't wait for anything but started pummeling him like fury, shouting for the maid and the cook. But even though I was big for my age, I wasn't much at fighting full-grown men. He gave my ear a box that made me see stars and then his elbow slammed my jaw, and I rolled away.

But I heard him jump up and run for the wall again. I leaped after him and tackled blindly, getting him by his waist and then sliding around his legs as he struggled away. I pulled back on his right leg and tripped him. Again he swatted me with his knuckles, this time rapping me on the head. Ahead of us, on the wall, a gun went off, and the man I was struggling with yelled, "No!"

At his yell, another gun went off across the yard. A bullet chipped off a piece of the overturned cement bench right behind us. I let go and rolled onto the grass, belly side up. Surprisingly, the man I'd just been tackling stopped, and his big hand groped along my shirt. I didn't give him a chance to find what he was looking for but smashed him with an uppercut that stunned him.

The man on the wall fired back at whoever was shooting across the yard at us, trying to pin down whoever was over there. Then I realized that whoever was over there was probably on *my* side, but they didn't know I was out on the lawn tussling with these two.

The guy I'd hit was getting up again, but I was too scared to move. He scurried off somewhere—not the wall; it was too dangerous. I knew I had to get away, too, because both sides kept shooting.

The tool shed was close by. I rolled over and stomached up to it, then crept inside. It smelled like damp wood and gasoline. Then I got an idea.

I groped around in the dark until I found a gasoline can. I shook it around and could hear that it was almost full.

I crawled to the door and poured a lot of it out on the dewy grass, then pulled off my undershirt behind cover of the shed door—where the white wouldn't show at all.

I unraveled part of the undershirt and lowered it into the can. Things were quiet for the moment on the lawn—everybody reloading, I guessed. I slid out the door and crawled around the back of the shed. I couldn't hear anybody back there hiding.

The tool shed was on the back corner of the lawn, close to the section on the wall where I guessed the man with the gun to be stationed. I had noticed when we drove in that the wall was in sections, with high stone posts jutting up about every ten feet. He was probably sheltered behind the top of one of the high posts.

I had matches with me. My heart hurt, because I knew both sides would see me when I lit one, and neither side would be sure of who I was. But I cupped one hand over the match, struck it, and lit the fuse. Then I ran behind the shed—just in time!

The gas can erupted with an explosion and a high sheet of flame, illuminating one man crouched on the wall behind a post, and another man racing across the lawn towards him.

It went out just as quickly, but there was instant gunfire—then silence. Sirens were blaring in the distance, coming closer. I heard the men slide off the wall and land on their feet on the other side. In spite of having fought them, I was glad they got away. That flame from the gas can had showed me something I hadn't expected to see. The man on the grass had been Tom Blancke—The Juggler.

People were running toward the tool shed, and lights were springing on in the big and elegant house.

As the police cars swept past the house, I heard my aunt calling, "Scruggs! Scruggs!"

I poked my head out from behind the shed. "Here I am!" I called in a whisper. "They got away."

"I know. It's all right. That was only Rick firing at them. We had no idea you were out here at first, until you lit the gas can."

I came out onto the lawn and joined her. It was easier to see, facing the house and its lights. Rick was scanning the yard, gun in hand.

"That was quick thinking," she told me, leaning on me as she trod to the house. I helped her along.

"Are you all right?" I asked her. "Did they scare you?"

Suddenly she laughed. "Oh Scruggs, there's more to your aunt than you know. If I had had a gun, I would have been firing away at them with Rick. And, unlike Rick, I wouldn't have missed. Don't worry, nephew, your aunt has nerves of steel!"

"Do you know who they were?" I asked.

"I am a wealthy woman. They were ready to rob me at gunpoint, that's all—but Rick is always ready for that sort of thing. Aren't you Rick?"

"You know it!" he exclaimed, coming up out of the darkness from his search. He punched my arm. "Sorry I almost hit you with a bullet, tiger. I didn't know you had the stomach to take on trouble like that. Good thinking with that gas can. Good thinking all right." And he wasn't smirking. As we got closer to the house, I could see that. I felt better, seeing that he liked me.

"I saw T—I saw that one guy looking in my window," I told them, "and I chased him. Then I heard the one on the wall start shooting. I think there were only two of them."

"Yes, just two," Rick agreed. "Cook has probably gone to bed. I'll have Janet make you something hot." Then when we stepped through the sliding doors into the living room, he whistled at me. "Look at that mug. Cut you up a bit with his hands. Janet, make some cocoa, would you?" he asked her.

She had come out in her robe and slippers. She took one look at me and disappeared into the kitchen.

Both my aunt and the chauffeur fussed over me and made me feel like a hero for what I'd done. They especially liked it that I'd struck the man—Tom Blancke, as I knew him—when he had bent over me.

"That's thinking," my aunt said. "Your wits don't leave you in a pinch, Scruggs."

"I should say not," Rick agreed with her. "Nor his guts, either. A fine fighter. We should take you up to the boxing gym, we should, and get you some training."

"Would you?" I asked my aunt.

She laughed. "If you want, nephew, but I think you'd better see how you feel tomorrow before you try it."

"True enough," Rick said, laughing. "The morning after a fight isn't very pleasant. Well, I'll patrol the grounds a bit, madam," he told her. "And by and by turn in, unless you want me to keep watch all night."

"No, Rick. Keep an eye out for a while, but I think they've gone for good—at least for the rest of the night."

"Aren't you going to call the cops back?" I asked.

He looked away and hid a grin, I thought. She smiled. "Oh, Scruggs, you are naive. The police could only hunt around. They wouldn't find anything. I prefer to rely on private means to solve these sorts of problems."

She made it sound like all rich people did that, so I just nodded like of course that was the logical thing.

Janet brought hot cocoa for us, and Rick went to patrol around before he retired for the night in the little house alongside the big one. I didn't say anything about Tom Blancke.

It seemed like neither my aunt nor Rick had gotten a look at his face—they had been quite a distance away. And Aunt Caroline didn't think to ask me. I felt uneasy inside. It was still hard to think that Tom was The Juggler I was supposed to beware of.

By the time I went to bed, my face—especially my jaw—was sore and stiff, and I knew I owed my bruises and black eye to Tom Blancke. But I lay in bed re-creating the whole scene—how I had chased him, how we had fallen. The guy on the wall had fired what I figured was a warning shot to get me away from Tom. I knew the guy on the wall had seen me silhouetted as I came out my bedroom window. He could have hit me easy right then if he had wanted to.

Then I thought of how I'd tackled Tom and heard the gunshot from across the lawn. As soon as I'd fallen, he had stopped running. I realized that Tom had figured I'd been hit. Right there in all that danger he had stopped to see where I was hurt. And I'd gone and cracked him one for his troubles. Still, he shouldn't have been trespassing and snooping around.

I felt sick inside—even though I guessed anybody in his right mind would punch a prowler. But it was too much all at once—the prowler, the cook, Chicken Kiev, a fight, a new place that was a mansion. And my aunt— old and frail and yet with iron nerves and something about her that seemed fierce.

Tomorrow's Sunday, I told myself. I'll call Mr. Birky and go to church with him . . . better call him early if he goes to church in the city. Then I fell asleep, and the first day was over.

## Chapter Eight
# Behind the Mask of Aunt Caroline

Sunlight was pouring into the room when I woke up. I started to sit up, but got stopped by a hundred hot needles in my legs and chest. With a groan I sank back. Last night's fight had settled, all right.

I gently touched my face, running my fingers up along my cheekbone and right eye. The eye was swollen, and the skin felt sensitive to pressure. I glanced at the clock. It said 12:30.

"Twelve-thirty!" I almost jumped up again, but caught myself before it hurt. Now I was sure Mr. Birky would think I'd been faking the people in Peabody along all this time. It would look like I didn't care two licks for Christianity or church.

"What a way to start," I moaned.

I swung my legs over the edge of the bed and stood up slowly. I switched on the clock radio by the bed to see if Tom and his partner had been caught during the night. But even though I found a news station, all I caught was some story about a laser crystal that had been stolen in San Jose and then the weather. No mention of any neighborhood prowlers in Palo Alto.

After a hot shower and a change of clothes, I decided I'd better find Mr. Birky's number and give him a call to explain myself and get a ride to evening church. I hunted around the room looking for where I'd thrown my clothes from the night before, but I couldn't find them. So I went into the hallway and snooped around until I found a clothes hamper in one of the linen closets. There were my pants and shirt on top of the pile. But nothing was in the pockets. They had been emptied.

I went back to the bedroom. On top of the bureau I found my wallet. The few dollars that I'd put in it were still there, but I couldn't find Mr. Birky's or Tom's number anywhere.

Just then somebody knocked.

"Come in," I said, and the maid walked in.

"I'm ready to clear the sideboard from breakfast," she said. "Would you like to eat first?"

"Yeah, sure. Thanks." I slipped my wallet into my pocket and followed her out.

Sunday breakfast was less formal than the evening meal had been. There were eggs, toast, sausages, bacon, bagels, cream cheese, and butter set out on the sideboard by the table. I got a plate and helped myself, and then poured a cup of coffee from the warming pot at the end.

Aunt Caroline walked in, bundled up as usual, but looking somehow fresh and alive, as though she'd been out enjoying herself. I figured she probably liked roses or something and had been gardening. From the little bit I'd seen driving in, gardening was a favorite pastime in wealthy Palo Alto.

"Why, nephew! Up at last?" she greeted me.

"Sorry I slept so long. Must have been from the fight last night."

"Quite a lovely shiner you've got."

"I missed church, too," I said grimly. "I didn't mean to do that."

Her eyes flicked over me carelessly. "Don't you think you're a little beyond that sort of thing?" she asked.

"No," I told her frankly. "Didn't you hear about my past? Seems like you'd want me in church."

"That's what I mean. Why would a boy with your . . . interests . . . drag yourself to church?"

"Because I'm not the same as I was," I began. "You see, about a year ago—" But she stopped me.

"No, no," she said, trying to sound careless but sounding urgent, too. "No, I see it all perfectly. You had a 'conversion,' didn't you? And then some kind little old man or lady took you in—made you feel all at home and just hung on every step you took toward joining the church and reforming yourself. Isn't that it?" She didn't wait for an answer. I was bridling up, but she either didn't notice or didn't care. "Yes, I see it is. You see, Scruggs, some people feel powerful when they amass money and wealth. Some people feel powerful when they—"

"When they help somebody else?" I cut in. "When they take care of somebody that never even knew what it was like—" But I cut myself off. I figured she would laugh if I said anything about love.

"They feel powerful when they win converts," she added smoothly. "I don't want you to be a victim of people like that."

"Mrs. Bennett wasn't that way," I told her. "And neither is Mr. Birky. Do you know what happened to the card he gave me?"

"I had Janet put your clothes in the hamper. If his card was in your pocket, she likely put it in the trash with the other papers."

I turned to go find Janet, but my aunt's voice stopped me. "And the trash is sent through the shredder every morning," she added. "I handle important papers and can't afford to leave them intact. I'm sorry if Janet inadvertently lost the number, but she did it in innocence." She helped herself to some coffee and sat at the table. "Why not eat your breakfast before it gets cold?"

Defeated, I sat across from her. My heart felt like a stone. Nobody had ever accused Mrs. Bennett like that before. I'd never thought about things like *why* she had helped me so much. Aunt Caroline seemed to read my thoughts.

"I had thought you were smarter than that, Scruggs," she said softly. "I had thought you never trusted anybody at all. That was what your caseworkers had indicated to me."

"I never did," I said. "Until last year. Those people at church seemed so different from everybody else."

"Dear me, you are naive. I never trust church people. They always want something. In fact, I make it my habit never to trust anybody."

Suddenly I hated her for saying that to me. I didn't care if it was a sin to talk back to her. "Then why should I trust you?" I asked her.

She leaned back and smiled. "Bravo, nephew. That's the attitude I like. Everybody, including me, has his little game to play. A smart person realizes that before he trusts those sincere, sweet little smiles of church people. However," she added, "I am wealthy and have friends. I don't need *you* for anything. So you can trust me. Remember, you are all alone in this world and don't belong to anybody—" I gritted my teeth on that—"so I think you had better at least *try* to trust me."

"I trust Mrs. Bennett, too," I told her, and started eating doggedly.

I heard her laugh. "I hate to see you hurt, Scruggs. But if you trust someone like that long enough, you'll find out the truth in the end. And your aunt will still be here to pick up the pieces. Excuse me." And she left me.

After breakfast I went to the study in my room and fished out my Bible. Then I read it for two hours without looking up once. There was something about this place— I was afraid she was right, and I didn't want her to be. But in the middle of all that money and calmness, she had seemed so assured.

After I'd read awhile, I set to figuring things out. I could remember Mrs. Bennett telling me that surely my aunt cared a lot to take me to live with her, sight unseen. And we'd known that my aunt had been told all about how bad I'd been.

Something didn't fit. I ran the morning's conversation through my mind again, as though I was telling Mrs. Bennett everything. I couldn't help thinking how Mrs. Bennett always called me "Son," trying to make me feel like we were family.

Then I paced a little, because I still felt those words from my aunt. *I didn't belong to anybody. I was alone. So I had to trust her.*

Then I thought about Mrs. Bennett and wished I were in Peabody.

Like I've said. I'm pretty dumb. It took me a while to figure things out. But then I did figure things out. When an aunt or foster mother loves you, she doesn't tell you you don't belong to anybody. She tells you that you belong to her. My mind flicked over to Mr. Birky. He'd done the same thing. "You call me Uncle Bill," he'd told me.

When an aunt takes you on sight unseen *because she loves you,* she doesn't laugh at you.

Nothing seemed to match with Aunt Caroline. Supposedly she had sent for me because she loved me— a big sacrifice for somebody who wasn't used to having a kid around. And she had promised the Agency to take care of me and be a mother to me.

I'll admit that the Children's Agency can't look into people's hearts, but they wouldn't have sent me out of the state unless they had been convinced that I would be well taken care of. They wouldn't have chosen Aunt Caroline sight unseen over Mrs. Bennett unless they had been *sure* that Aunt Caroline loved me and wanted to help me. Miss Stevens, even though she didn't believe the Bible and all that, had liked how I'd been changing since becoming a Christian. She, for one, wouldn't have wanted me to leave Peabody if she'd thought that Aunt Caroline was so . . . cold-blooded.

So maybe this lady named Aunt Caroline was hiding something. She had enough money to fake anything, from the looks of things. And she'd had the talent to fake the Agency. Maybe she wasn't even my aunt.

That idea kind of stuck with me. For one thing, my real father—who she said was her brother—had been dirt poor. So how did she end up so rich?

For another thing, there was that cold-blooded side of her—staying so calm and cheerful through a gunfight.

And then the way she had reacted to Mr. Birky and Tom Blancke at the airport. Like she was hiding me from them, trying to keep me away.

I wanted to go to church that night, but Mr. Birky's phone number wasn't listed in the telephone book, so I didn't even bother asking if I could go. I was pretty sure Aunt Caroline would have figured out some way of preventing me if I had asked.

I checked my wallet again and found Mrs. Bennett's address still tucked inside. I sat down at the desk but couldn't find any paper, so I tore the flyleaf out of one of my books and wrote:

Dear ~~Mrs. Bennett~~ Mother,

I miss you a lot. My aunt—if that's who she is—doesn't want me to go to church or make friends with anybody except her chauffeur and the maid. Please ask Miss Stevens to check up on her and make sure she really is my aunt. In a way she scares me. Today she told me that I am alone and don't belong to anybody, so I have to trust her.

If it turns out that she really is my aunt but has some strange ideas, that's okay. But I think Miss Stevens ought to check. Otherwise, everything is okay. The food is good, and last night I got into a fight, so I felt more at home. Please send me the address and phone number of Jack's Uncle Bill. I lost it and can't find it. He met me at the airport.

Write soon. I am praying to be your son more than ever.

Love,
~~Scruggs~~
William

Mrs. Bennett never liked my nickname, even though it's what I call myself. I can't get used to William or even Bill after ten years or more of "Scruggs." But I'm glad she doesn't use it. Somehow seems more personal when she uses my real name. I crossed out "Scruggs" and wrote "William" in its place.

I couldn't find an envelope in the desk, but I found some tape, so I folded my letter up to envelope size and taped it shut. Then I addressed it, and hunted for stamps. But I couldn't find those either.

There was no point in asking for a stamp, because I didn't want anybody to know I was mailing the letter. I kept it under my shirt for the rest of the day, and that night I slipped it into one of the pillowcases on the bed and didn't move my head off it. If it killed me, that letter was getting back to Peabody.

## Chapter Nine
# The Secret Letter

Somehow I had a funny idea about that hot chocolate from the night before. Maybe, I told myself, I was being too imaginative, but maybe there was some medical reason for having slept so late. On Sunday night I turned down a hot drink and went straight to bed.

I can sleep all keyed up and alert, and sort of time myself to get up when I want to. Before I went to bed, I told myself I had to be up at five, and sure enough, at five minutes until five, my eyes snapped open, and I lay tense in the dark, trying to remember what I was supposed to do.

Then it came back to me, and I crawled out of bed. I'd slept with the door locked, and everything was the way it had been the night before. I slipped on trousers and a shirt, and then eased open the window.

It was dark in the walled-in yard, but beyond the wall the sky was lightening from navy blue to blue tinged with red.

I heard someone cough, and I froze. It was only Rick going by, doing a round of the yard.

Why? I asked myself. I wondered if he was guarding the house from anybody coming in, or anybody breaking out. But he didn't seem tense or very alert, just wandering around like a guy who's sure everything is okay for the last stretch of the night. I figured he was wondering how soon it would be till breakfast.

He went past without detouring to check the tool shed and disappeared from the back light's reach on the other side of the house. I slipped out the window. Tom and his buddy had been using a rope the night they'd come over, or so I figured. The wall was a little high to scale without help. I slipped up my side of the yard and climbed over the slats of the locked wooden gate.

Then I dropped down on the other side and pelted up the street to where I remembered the highway had been. After that I sort of wandered along, watching for an all-night store or maybe a milk-and-gas place that opened early.

After about a half hour of roaming, I found my way to just such a place, and they had a stamp machine. I got change for a dollar, got a stamp, and fixed it onto my letter.

"Is there a mailbox?" I asked the guy at the register.

"Down the road," he told me, jerking his thumb toward the highway outside. I followed the road until I came to the box and dropped the letter inside. Mission accomplished. Time to go home.

The sun finished coming up as I headed homeward. The tall palm trees along the highway were becoming less like moptop shadows and more like trees. Aunt Caroline seemed like the type to be up with the dawn, so as soon as I walked in, she would probably have a million questions. I wanted to make up some story to feed her, but I decided against it. Maybe, I told myself, she'll get mad at me and send me back to the Agency. Then at least I can go to Peabody again, even if I have to stay in a group home.

But when I climbed over the fence again, cut along the house, and came in through my window, everything was the way I had left it.

I didn't feel like sleeping, so I showered and dressed again, then came out to see if breakfast was ready. By then it was almost seven.

"Ah, Scruggs," my aunt greeted me in the dining room. "Breakfast is being prepared. You look wide awake and fresh this morning. In a better temper, I hope?"

"Yes," I told her.

"Not going to spend the day sulking in your room, eh?"

"No, aunt."

"Good. I thought I might take you into the city today—visit some of the sights. How does that sound?"

"Sounds great—uh, but—"

"Yes?"

"Shouldn't I be going to school?"

"Oh, school, yes. Well, Scruggs, school is another thing that money can handle. I thought we would begin our vacation about a month early, and in September, I can have you enrolled just as easily into your next grade. Some of the private schools around here are just marvelously . . . flexible."

I gave a brief nod. Now I knew she'd been faking the Agency along. I've played hooky so much in my life, the Agency would never have put me where that kind of thing would be allowed. They wanted me *in* school, and they would have grilled Aunt Caroline on that point.

"Have some coffee," she told me. "I hope that yesterday's pout helped you end your little game of church. Did it?"

"No," I told her frankly. "I still want to go."

She drummed her fingertips on the table. "A person only plays with me for so long, Scruggs."

"I'm not playing with you," I told her—only I was thinking about what Mrs. Bennett had told me about martyrs. This lady, whoever she was, had sent for me all the way from Peabody. She wanted something, and under that veil of middle-aged politeness, I could see that she would do anything to get it.

She got up and left the table very suddenly and was gone a few minutes, but when she came back, she was in control of herself. "I do love a good contest of wills," she told me, "only because I never lose them. Let church be our bone of contention. A harmless enough bone, to be sure."

Then Janet came out with breakfast, and we ate.

"Lack of religion hasn't hurt your appetite," my supposed aunt said.

"I don't *have* to be in church," I told her. "Christianity doesn't depend on that."

"Spare me the morning devotions, please." She glanced up at Janet, and Janet disappeared. We ate the rest in silence. But I had some uneasy feeling.

After we'd finished, she said, "I'm going to send you and Rick to Giarhdelli Square together. You are to stay with him, but you may go wherever you please. He will do whatever you want. Here is fifty dollars. Go on now, and tell him you're ready to go."

"Thank you," I said, and stood up.

"Just do me a favor and spend it all. Maybe some filthy lucre will open your eyes." That was her idea of a joke.

Rick had his leer back on when I found him in the servant's quarters, but by then I knew how to soften him up. I talked about the fight in the yard on Saturday night, and then got him to talking about fights that he had been in.

On the way into the city I sat in the front with him because I felt too stupid sitting alone in the back. He had a good time telling me about this fight and that.

I could see that this guy was no more a chauffeur than I was. He'd been a drifter, a fighter, and I guessed from some things that he said, he'd been involved with crooks and thugs from way back.

Well, I might be dumb about a lot of things, but it was a good thing that Rick was dumber. He had no idea what I was figuring out from his fight stories. One thing was sure, he was working for Aunt Caroline for the money, which was another thing that told me he was no chauffeur. That was just a thing on the side—a cover.

We parked in a parking garage near the square and walked down to it. Giarhdelli Square sits opposite the wharf. I'd never seen anything like it. Black carriages pulled by sleek black or brown horses rattled past every few minutes. On the wharf side of the road there was a park with old-fashioned cable cars lined up for business. Then along the sidewalk in front of the park were all sorts of tables set up, full of T-shirts, sweatshirts, jewelry, jade, wooden musical instruments, carvings, and paintings. Some players sat opposite the tables. They sat on a brick dike that bordered the park. One man would play his harmonicas. Another man had a guitar. He was a middle-aged black man with a squashed cap on his head and a grizzled beard. I liked him. He could play anything I asked him to. He knew all sorts of songs, and he wanted the people watching him to sing with him.

I felt too shy, but some of the other people sang. Then there was a man who juggled, and two men who did imitations. Rick laughed at me for being so amazed at these guys. All of them had a little felt hat somewhere nearby, and people who watched the performers would throw money into the hats.

"Beggars!" Rick called them. "Lowest form of life!"

But I liked them. And it looked to me like honest work, which was more than I thought Rick had done in his time. Then we went back across the street and into Giarhdelli Square.

Chocolate was everywhere. Rick gave me a full tour of the place. He showed me a store called Stevie's Sweeties, and I bought some chocolates to take back to Aunt Caroline. I figured if she'd given me fifty bucks, the least I could do was take her a present back. Rick laughed again when I told him that.

"You sure are a sweet boy," he told me so that the lady at the cash register heard him. "Taking your little old aunt a present, eh?" Then he burst out laughing again. I felt my face burning red. Blushing as usual!

"You leave him alone!" the lady at the register said. "I get hundreds of kids a day that only say,'Gimme, gimme, gimme.' I think it's nice he's taking his aunt something."

"Yeah, he's a nice boy, all right," Rick said with his usual leer. "Good Sunday-school kid—ah well, no hard feelings between you and me, Scruggs. I know you're a good fighter when you get your dander up."

The lady handed me the bag with my candy in it for Aunt Caroline, and she said, "I do hope you'll come back, sir. It's been a pleasure." And she glared at Rick like she was thinking the same thing I was thinking. She and I got to talking. Her name was Maxine Sugar, and she and her husband ran their own business there. I liked Mrs. Sugar because she was nice, and I was glad to stand there chatting while Rick fumed to get me away. He didn't like me to make friends.

After Giarhdelli Square, Rick took me down to Fisherman's Wharf, and we saw some of the boats all tied up. He told me he was going to own one someday—not a fishing boat but a nice little yacht. I could have pressed him for some information on how he planned to get rich, but I got distracted. There was just too much to see. This time it was a guy dressed up like a pirate—I mean really dressed up. He wasn't wearing any five-and-dime phoney costume, but real over-the-knee boots, a black leather jerkin, knotted kerchief—the works. He had a cutlass in a scabbard, and there were all kinds of flintlock pistols shoved through his belt and in and out of his jerkin.

The best thing was the parrots he had—big, blazing colored ones. Some of them talked and whistled. One sat on each shoulder, and one was perched on a mailbox by him. There were two others he was showing to some tourists.

The pirate walked with a rolling walk, and he talked like Long John Silver. For any amount of money, he would let you have your picture taken with him. But we didn't have a camera.

"Maybe we could come back with one some day," I told Rick. He laughed at me. "So you want a camera, Scruggs? Follow me!" And he led me into a store about three doors down. He bought a little instamatic and some batteries. Then he loaded it up and handed it to me.

"Now go get your photos," he told me. "And don't forget how much money can buy!"

## Chapter Ten

# What Money Can Buy

The guy dressed like a pirate let me hold the parrots and play around with them as much as I wanted to. I kept slipping dollar bills to him, just to make it worth his while. Then we posed, and Rick took four pictures of us.

It was purely inspiration, but suddenly I asked him, "Is there anybody around here named The Juggler?"

"Ah mate, there's dozens of the lubbers!" he told me, staying in character. "Jugglers everywhere from Pier 39 to the tip of Giarhdelli Square! But the best one's in the Cannery."

He was right about that. Finding somebody called "The Juggler" in San Francisco was like trying to find somebody called O'Malley in Ireland. There were jugglers everywhere—right alongside the guitar players and mimes and the pirate. Most of the street minstrels could juggle, and I got the idea that juggling was the easiest way a person could break into the street performing that was so popular along the Fisherman's Wharf.

Then Rick took my arm and said there was plenty more to see. He hadn't heard me ask the pirate about

The Juggler. I didn't trust Rick enough to pump him on that score.

We visited Pier 41 and then found a teriyaki place for lunch. Talk about fancy. Rick kept laughing at me every time I seemed impressed. For one thing, I didn't think we were dressed right for a fancy place, but he waved it away and called for the host to seat us. "You watch," he told me, winking. "It's money. Money does it, Scruggs." And the host seated us.

We made a fair start on Pier 39, but there were so many things to see and watch, that we didn't cover everything. Pier 39 is kind of like a boardwalk, except it has a second floor to it, which is also a boardwalk. I'd bought a couple sweatshirts, soft pretzels, and some popcorn, and Rick had kept up pretty well with the purchases. But at last he said we'd better go home and get some dinner. The chef didn't like it if people missed their meals at home. It insulted him.

We found the parking garage, threw our stuff into the back seat, and started the hour ride home. Rick turned on the radio and found a classical station for me. "Never thought you'd listen to this stuff," he said.

"A friend back home started me on it," I told him without bothering to explain it had been Mrs. Bennett. I didn't feel like hearing another lecture.

Then the news came on, and the story about the stolen laser crystal was still the top story.

"Smart dogs!" Rick said with a snort that I figured meant approval.

"Sounds like they just upset the whole nation's defense," I said. "That crystal was going to be put into the Strategic Defense Initiative up in space."

He glanced at me out of the side of his eyes. "Oh, you've been following the news. Guess it was. Too bad those brass heads didn't use a little strategic defense when they invented the thing. Anybody stupid enough to leave it out deserves to lose it."

I didn't answer him. Instead, I changed the subject. "Did you mean it when you said I should learn to box?" I asked him.

"Sure I did. Just ask your aunt if you can."

"I think I will. Do you go to a gym anywhere?"

"Nah. I know enough boxing to spin anybody's head around." Then he was off telling me about all his fights again, and while he talked, I let myself think about Mrs. Bennett and the letter. I hoped it would reach her in two days instead of three.

Aunt Caroline—I still called her that—was surprised at the candy I brought her, but not in the way Mrs. Bennett would have been surprised—thanking me and making a big fuss about it. Aunt Caroline was just plain old surprised, like she had discovered something else about me that she hadn't expected.

But she seemed to want to be friends, and she didn't mention church. She liked the sweatshirts I'd picked out and had me try them on, and she sent Rick out with the film, even though the roll wasn't finished.

"I'm so glad that you're learning how to enjoy being rich," she told me. "Isn't it fun?"

I shrugged and gave her a half-nod so that she wouldn't be mad. I would have traded the whole day for a plane ticket back to Peabody, but I didn't say that.

After dinner and after she had finished making a fuss over the trip, I went to my room to go to bed. I put the shirts away and flung myself into the chair in my study. After hearing about nothing but fights and money all day, I was ready to read my Bible. I had never in my life felt so ready to read it. But when I put my hand on the floor by the recliner, I only felt carpet. I looked down. The Bible was gone.

I looked under the chair and behind it and went through the desk drawers and checked all the shelves of the bookcase. It was definitely gone.

I don't care, I told myself savagely. I'll buy another one.

Then my heart stabbed me at the thought that money might solve even that problem. Money, money—suddenly everything was money.

"I hate money!" I yelled. "I hate it, and I hate these shirts and everything else!" And without thinking I grabbed up the nearest book and flung it right through my window.

It was a stupid thing to do, but a rage had a hold of me, and when my aunt burst in, I yelled, "Where is my Bible? What did you do with it?"

"Rick, control that boy," she said calmly. He half-tackled me, then got behind me and held me pinned in with his arms, but I was smart enough not to fight with him. I let him hold me in that bear hug from behind. But I felt my face burning red with rage, and I had to gulp my breath, fighting to yell and not cry all at the same time.

"You are a child," she told me. That brought my voice back.

"You aren't my aunt!" I screamed at her. "I know you aren't! I'm not so dumb I can't figure it out! Let me out of here!"

I felt Rick tense, but she stayed cool and calm. "If you aren't quiet, I'll have you gagged until you are."

Then I stopped and just stood there, heaving and panting.

"I am your aunt," she told me. "I'm the only friend you have right now."

"Oh no you aren't," I told her. "We aren't kin. You couldn't care less about me. Somehow or another you found out about me—some punky kid with all the makings of a crook. That's what you want me for."

Even she drew back. I hadn't realized what I'd been saying, and I was as surprised as anybody. But it did make sense. Rick had been spending the whole day trying to teach me to do anything I could for money. That's what made it so apparent. I'd been too dumb to realize it until just then, with my blood going and adrenaline up.

"You will be punished for breaking that window," she told me. "You will stay in this room until you apologize and acknowledge the truth—that I am your aunt. If Rick catches you trying to get out, it will be the worse for you. Let him go, Rick."

He threw me onto the bed, and they walked out. I had never noticed that my door locked on the outside. Maybe if I had, I would have been more careful. I heard her lock it, and I was alone.

But the rage was past. I sobbed some real hard sobs of anger and then stopped. The first thing I did after I was calm was to find my pocket New Testament that I'd packed with my shirts. She hadn't thought about getting that.

Then I sat down to think. It all came down to figuring out who she really was, and how she knew about me. The only crook I'd ever even heard of was that Tom Thumb lady that Jack and Penny had tangled with a year ago. She had been a smuggler, which fit with Aunt Caroline, but why would she care about me? I figured it was unlikely she'd ever even heard about me.

One thing was clear—she was a desperate person. I had to escape.

## Chapter Eleven
# What Money Can't Buy

They brought me food three times a day—straight from the cook. It looked to me like Aunt Caroline was still trying to act like she was my real aunt. On Tuesday morning Rick fixed the window I'd broken.

Otherwise, there was silence between them and me until Friday, when She came in, all wrapped up in her shawls and bent over. She had a letter for me—unopened. She thrust it to me. Rick was standing behind her, arms crossed, ready in case I tried to get away.

The stationery was Mrs. Bennett's. I opened the letter and read it:

Dear Scruggs,

I got your letter and was sorry to find out how unhappy you are, but I think that you must try to work at liking California. Please obey your aunt and be good for her. Do what she tells you.

You must learn to cut the cords with your past and begin your life out there. I think it would be best if you stopped writing me for a while and concentrated on the present. I should hope that a good Christian boy would be grateful for the chance of an education and travel.

Love,
Mrs. Bennett

At first, the letter hit me like a brick. Then I forced myself to look up at their satisfied faces.

"So she has let you go," Aunt Caroline said. "I knew she would. I told you that these church people are all alike."

"Nice fake job," I said, handing it back to her. "You're a real pro. You even got the stationery right." What she'd gotten wrong was the "Dear Scruggs."

"Poor Scruggs. You still don't believe me, do you?" she asked.

"Sorry, no. You aren't my aunt any more than Rick is. And you had better keep a close guard on me, lady, because as soon as I can, I'm getting out of here."

Her sympathy turned hard. "I will give you another day," she told me. "And then, poor, dear Scruggs, I will have to take you to a psychiatrist—who, I am sure, will provide ample medication to make you more docile. Poor recalcitrant Scruggs. You've picked a hard course, when you might have had your aunt's approval and affection from the very start."

Then they locked me in again. For the first time, I had a definite hunch about things. I went into my things and took out my envelope of scraps. The way I've figured it, tough guys don't keep scrapbooks. That's for girls. But I manage to stuff everything I want to keep into an old manila envelope.

I went into it and looked through the clippings I'd cut out from the Peabody papers until I found the clippings about Jack and Penny. There was one article that ran a whole story about that lady—Susan Walters, alias Tom Thumb.

I found an eraser in the desk and rubbed out a lot of the hair in the newspaper picture they had of her. It was just a mug shot, but it had been pretty recent. The eraser whitened the hair. Then I drew some shawls on her shoulders to build them up, and I put some shadows on her face. It was nothing that some powder and a little bit of make-up couldn't do on a real face every morning.

I found myself looking at a photograph of my "aunt."

"So that's who you are," I mumbled. I felt better—tons better. Now I knew for sure I didn't owe her anything. If I could just escape, I could go home—home to Mrs. Bennett and a real home.

If I could escape—that was a big if.

I flung myself on top of the bed, fully dressed as usual. Since being locked up, I hadn't felt at ease enough to be anything else but perfectly ready.

I had been sleeping lightly, but that night I fell into a deep sleep. I guess a guy can only go so long without it.

When I woke up, the sun was out, and She and Rick were by my bed. They let me sit up.

"You have a letter to write," she told me.

"I do?" I asked.

"Yes. You will be sending these photographs of you and the pirate to your dear Mrs. Bennett, and you will tell her that you got her letter and are beginning to adjust."

"Sure," I told her. I sat at the desk and wrote on a piece of paper that she gave me.

Dear Mother,

    I'm being held prisoner by a lady who isn't even my aunt. She wants to turn me into a crook. Send help.

Love,
Scruggs

Then I handed it to her.

"Oh, bravo, Scruggs," she told me, and handed the letter to Rick. "Have a letter made from that handwriting, Rick. Make it say what we had planned, and don't forget to include the photos."

Tricked again! I set my teeth. It was obvious they had gotten Mrs. Bennett's real answer and had hired some forger to copy the penmanship to fool me. All they had wanted was a sample of my penmanship to do the same thing to her.

Rick left with a brief nod. "No tricks, Scruggs. I think we understand each other," she told me. "If I were really some cruel kidnaper who had spirited you out here, do you know what I might do?" she asked me.

"Go on, tell me. I hate riddles," I said.

"I would tell you that I know all about your precious Mrs. Bennett, and I have it in my power to do her any amount of harm I choose. But since I am your aunt, I wouldn't do that." Then she smiled sweetly at me. "Do we go to the psychiatrist today, Scruggs, or have you seen the light?"

"I've seen the light all right," I told her and jumped at her. She nimbly jumped back, which was just what I wanted. My jump brought me up to the bookcases. I set my shoulder to the one on the end and with one motion knocked it over into the study. It didn't hit her, but it fell against the desk, making a blockade between us which she couldn't scramble over very fast. Not as fast as I went out that window.

I shielded my face with my arms and flew out through the splintering glass. Then I pelted across the grass. Rick had heard the crash and was coming in the gate along the side of the house. We raced to the tool shed, and I got there first. With a heave I lifted myself up and climbed it to the roof.

From the roof it was a short jump to the wall that surrounded the yard. I made it while that lug was climbing the shed. Then he jumped for it and missed, falling short and sliding down the wall. I leaped down to the sidewalk below and hightailed it out of there.

I had to find Mr. Birky, but fast!

First I sprinted to the highway and crossed it. Then I tore over lawns, through yards, looking for more highways to cross with plenty of red lights. I hoped that would be the longest route for them if they followed me.

At last I stopped behind a store and felt my face. It was bleeding from bits of glass. So were the backs of my hands. I had to wash them and get the glass out. Now that I'd stopped running, I could feel the pain from the splinters smarting in my forehead and cheeks.

I found a fast-food place with restrooms on the outside, went in, and washed my face as gently as I could. The old bruises had been healing just fine until this. It took a lot more nerve than I thought I had, but I went over the cuts one by one, picking out the glass. There wasn't as much as I'd thought there might have been.

After that I washed myself harder, to see if I felt any glass, but I didn't, so I left.

I asked a guy how to get to Mountain View, and happily, it wasn't very far. Kind of right next door to Palo Alto.

It took me an hour and a half to get there, walking and hiding, but I made it.

I found an outdoor phone booth and looked up attorneys in the phone book. I had already looked once for his name and hadn't found it, but now I looked through the listings for law firms. There were only three that listed the business name without listing the names of all the partners. I memorized the addresses and started off. My hunch was, he was employed in one of those places.

The first place I stepped into smelled like old books and finely polished leather. A secretary gave me an eye-over and asked if she could help me. I told her I was in trouble and was looking for a Mr. Bill Birky who had promised to help me.

"I don't know a Mr. Birky," she told me. "But I believe my employer does," and she buzzed somebody from a back office, then said something into her telephone receiver. It must have been an intercom to the back.

A minute later a tall, young-looking lawyer came out of the back. He shook my hand and told me he was a friend of Mr. Birky's. He gave me Mr. Birky's home phone number and his business number. Then he let me call from the office phone.

Was I ever relieved to hear that voice on the other end!

"That you, Bill Grady?" he asked me over the line. "Where are you?"

I told him, and he said, "My practice is in the city. That's why you couldn't find my number in Mountain View. I live in Mountain View, and my home phone is unlisted. Hang on tight. I'm coming to get you."

Then he hung up, and the secretary brought me some coffee. I took it and sank down into a leather-covered chair.

## Chapter Twelve
# My First Uncle

Mr. Birky (he kept telling me to call him Uncle, but I couldn't get used to it) came within an hour.

"Looks like you been scrappin'," he told me after we'd climbed into his new-smelling Cutlass Supreme.

"Went through a window," I told him. "They didn't rough me up very much, just kind of kept me prisoner once I told them the score."

He nodded. "Well, it's time for the police to investigate, son."

"Do you think I could go home soon?" I asked him.

He smiled. "California can be a great place when you aren't being held captive by smugglers—if that's who they really are."

"I can prove to you that my 'Aunt Caroline' is Susan Walters," I told him. "I don't know about the rest. Have you got the old newspaper clippings about Jack and Penny?"

"I have photocopies," he told me.

"That'll do. Besides," I said, getting back to the first subject. "I really just want to go home to Peabody. Jack and Penny can keep the mysteries."

He nodded and gave my shoulder a rub. "I know it hasn't been easy for you. Did they threaten you all along?"

"No, sir. They tried to buy me off. And they tried to talk me out of church. It wasn't until I blew my temper that they got rougher. I broke a window." And on saying that I kind of shifted uncomfortably. Getting away from them would have been a lot easier if I hadn't gone on a rampage. "I do that when I get mad," I told Mr. Birky. "I bust windows. I'm sorry about it afterward, but I still do it sometimes. Maybe you should know that before you take me in."

He grinned broadly. "Anger," he said. "A sign of immaturity. Youth." He looked out the window at the places along Rengstorff. "I'm an old man now," he told me. "Pushing sixty. Used to have a hot temper like you."

"How'd you get over it?" I asked.

"I paid for it, for one thing," he told me. "It made me grow up, but when it came right down to it, I learned how much the Lord loved me, and that carried me through the hard times. You'll learn; the Lord isn't finished with you. I just hope you don't suffer too much from your temper while you're learning."

At last we pulled into the driveway of an elegant little stucco house. He ushered me inside and introduced his wife as Aunt Betty.

"This is Bill Grady," he told her. "My namesake. Say hello to your aunt, Bill." And so to them I was Bill— not Scruggs—the namesake of Bill Birky.

"Look at that face!" she exclaimed. "You march into the bathroom, young man. I'll get the first-aid kit and be right there."

There isn't anything to say when some little old lady is fussing over you, wiping your face like you're a kid and scolding you for scrapping.

"I don't think you understand the seriousness of the situation," I tried to tell her.

"Stuff and nonsense, sir! I know you boys! Fight and fight! Scrap and scrap! Now you sit still. Every boy thinks that *his* fight is important!"

"But—"

"Sit still, sir! I'm almost through. You squirm so much a person would think I was killing you."

"But—"

Mr. Birky stuck his head in the open doorway. "The boy's been held prisoner, Betty," he told her; then to me, he added, "I just called the police, Little Bill."

"Little Bill! Wait a minute!" I jumped up but she pushed me back down.

"Of course, 'Little Bill'! How else will we tell you two apart when people are speaking," she told me. "Now sit still and be good! There! You look like the mummy from the tomb. Go into the kitchen. I know I have something I can whip up for lunch."

I didn't bother to protest any more. Sooner or later I'd be going home, and nobody would ever know anybody called me "Little Bill."

Mrs. Birky hit the kitchen like a well-trained whirlwind, flying here and there from pantry to cupboard while she cooked and asked me questions.

"Held you prisoner! How did you escape? Never mind— I see how: through the window. Well, it's high time my Bill took a hand in things. Oh, there you are," she said to him. "What have you found?"

"This photocopy of an article about that lady smuggler the kids ran into last year," he told her. He handed it to me. I asked him if he had any chalk, and he brought me some. Then I whited out her hair with it and used it and some pencil to change her face a little. Then I built up her shoulders again with shawls.

"Aren't you the whiz kid!" he exclaimed, looking at it. "That is your 'Aunt Caroline.' Question is, what'd she want you for?"

"All I can figure is that they've got the law after them," I said. "They must have needed me to do something for them."

"Good thought," he told me. "Old Susan Walters is losing her usefulness by having her mug run in the newspapers. So maybe she wanted to take you into the business. You say you didn't have any family, Little Bill?"

"No."

He walked away, looking down at the piece of paper, and I could see him tossing things around in his head, but Mr. Birky was too nice to say it. I had no family and a bad record with the Children's Agency. Somehow she'd gotten wind of me, and she knew that once she got me out of Wisconsin, there wouldn't be anybody in the world responsible for me. It would have been easy for her to have a few things faked, throw some money around, act like an innocent rich lady, and con the Agency into giving me to her—especially if she could prove we were related.

"Who will you go to back in Wisconsin?" Mr. Birky asked me.

"Mrs. Marie Bennett put in a bid to take me once," I told him. "We've been writing. She would take care of me."

"I'll call the airline," he told me, "and get you back home tomorrow."

I knew a ticket would cost hundreds of dollars, and I didn't have more than ten in my wallet.

"I could work for you first," I told him.

He laughed. "Don't worry about it." Then he told me that Jack and Penny would be coming out in a few days if I wanted to wait around for them, but I told him I wanted to go home.

"Sure, I understand," he said with a grin. "Ain't no place like home, right? You don't have no sand in your shoes."

"Not any more," I told him.

He called his travel agent while I was eating lunch. At last he looked up with his usual grin. "Eight A.M.!" he exclaimed. "We'll pack you off for home first thing in the morning!"

I sat back and sighed. Sure, I was scared to fly, but I couldn't wait to get back home.

Then while we were still eating, the police came and heard the whole story, and I showed the officers the done-up photocopy of Susan Walters. The first cops who came were stumped by it, but then they called one of their superiors, and he came and heard the story. Then they got hooked up to the police in San Jose and were talking with some bigwigs, and pretty soon the whole house was full of this officer and that officer, asking questions and figuring things out.

Mrs. Birky went half out of her head feeding everybody and making them at home while they worked and telling them not to light their cigars under *her* roof. The guys with the cigars looked real sheepish and put them away.

"About time somebody scolded them for it," she muttered.

"Well," Lieutenant Somebody-or-Other said at last while everybody gathered up notes and tape recorders, "I guess we've got everything we can from this young man, since he won't stay out here for more questioning—"

"Absolutely not!" Mr. Birky said. "He wants to go home, and he is! The ticket's been arranged!"

"Mmmm. Well, we've had a hunch the Walters gang was connected with that laser crystal that got stolen in

San Jose. It appears like they can't unload it very conveniently now that we're on to them. It's my guess they were hoping the boy would do it, either unwittingly or as an accomplice."

"How?" I asked.

"Oh, there are plenty of ways," he told me. "We're keeping an eye on the spy activity as much as we can, but Walters knows we would have been fooled if an unknown agent—you, in this case—had stepped in and made the connection with a buyer somehow. You probably would have slipped right past us. We aren't in the market for kid spies. She could have had you change jackets with someone or even spit the thing out in a wad of gum."

"Well, now it's up to you, Officer," Mr. Birky said. "Let me know if I can help you in any way."

The officer stood up and shook hands with us.

"Dinner time," Mrs. Birky said when they had all left.

After dinner I was beat. Mr. Birky told me the guest room was at the top of the stairs and to go on and make myself comfortable.

I showered and checked the tape on my face. Pretty ugly mess, really. I got into a robe Mr. Birky had lent me, and then crossed the hall to my room.

It was dark by this time, and the light switch didn't seem to work. I crossed inside to check the lamp, and the door quietly swung shut and clicked.

"Don't move." I'd have known Rick's voice anywhere.

## Chapter Thirteen

# Pier 39

Susan Walters, Rick, and Janet were standing around me when the lights came on. Susan Walters had dropped the Aunt Caroline routine. She was still dressed the same, but she stood erect, and for the first time I could see through the make-up on her face.

"I found your piece of artwork," she told me. "It was very foolish of you to have left it lying around."

"I don't like masquerade parties," I told her. "I never have. Why don't you take the gunk off your face and act serious?"

Her eyes narrowed. She didn't like being laughed at. But instead of saying anything, she just looked at Rick. He thrust a bundle of clothes at me. "Put these on."

"We'll be out back," she said. "If you want these Sunday-school friends of yours to make it to church next week, you'll be quiet." She and Janet went out the window—cool and calm, like they had done it a thousand times. From the window it was just a step to the garage roof, which sloped down enough to let somebody hang off and drop down.

I changed from the borrowed robe into the T-shirt, jeans, and black vinyl jacket that he handed me. The clothes I had been wearing were in tatters from going through the window. I donned my own running shoes.

Then he told me to come on and pushed me out the open window ahead of him. We walked across the garage roof and swung down into the yard below.

"All right," she said. "We've lost our tails for the time being. There's still time enough to make the exchange and clear out. We'll have to hurry. They may know all the places."

By "places" I figured she meant hiding places.

"What about The Juggler?" Rick asked. She shook her head when she saw that I recognized that name. So The Juggler, whoever he was, was teamed up with them.

They hustled me out of the yard and up the street to a car. It wasn't the limo this time, just a green hatchback. We had to squeeze into it.

"You steal this car?" I asked.

"Airport parking," Rick told me with a smirk. "It won't be missed for a week."

"Be quiet," Susan Walters snapped at him. He and I were in the back, and Walters and Janet were in the front. I looked at Janet, who had been quiet all this time.

"Are you really teamed up with these creeps?" I asked her.

This time Rick backhanded me in the mouth and told me to shut up. Janet didn't look at me. Walters glanced back as she drove. "Don't bruise him any more, Rick. We don't want him fainting at the pier."

From what she said, I thought they meant to take me for a swim with cement boots on. She laughed when she glanced back and saw me go pale. "Pier 39," she told me. "Nothing more dangerous than a video arcade, Scruggs.

All you have to do is walk inside, and somebody else will take care of the rest. Give him the quarters, Rick."

Rick thrust a roll of quarters at me. "Put them in your pants pocket," he ordered.

"Look," she said as she swung the car onto Highway 101 and headed for the city. "You go in that arcade, and you play out the roll of quarters. That's all. We'll be watching you the whole time. At the end of the night, you can call the cops, call the manager, call anybody. We'll let you go, and you can forget everything. Just do what we say now. Go in there and play out that roll of quarters. You'll have fifty arcade games to choose from."

"I don't get it," I told her.

"As long as you don't get it, you're safe. If you try to get away or call for help before you use up those quarters, we'll go in with our guns and take you out for a long swim. We'll be watching you the whole time you play."

After that she was silent. We drove past signs for Los Altos, Stanford, Redwood City, past restaurants, hotels, the San Francisco airport, until at last I could see the lighted mountainsides of the city. I'd never seen so many houses and buildings all together, all on the hills like that. At first it made me think of waves on some kind of shimmery sea; then somehow it made me think of postcards of Christmas villages, all lit up and make-believe.

But after a mile or so more, we were fighting city traffic, and the prettiness was gone. Walters swung in and out and around traffic, muttering under her breath, while Janet hung on and Rick kept one hand on the back of my collar, like he thought I might try to get away.

At last we were on Van Ness, back on the steep hills around the Wharf. She found a parking garage, and we walked down by Giarhdelli Square again, about a quarter mile up from the Pier.

"A nice scenic walk," she said in my ear. "Just because you can't see our guns, don't act like we don't have them."

"I'm not doing any fighting," I told her. We walked past the crab and oyster stands, past the teriyaki place, past Pier 41 and the horse and carriage rides, and then onto the boardwalk of Pier 39. There are plenty of little doorways and alcoves along the stores and restaurants built there. In places, these are overshadowed by the upper tier of the boardwalk. At that time of night, some of the smaller places were closed. Their dark doorways looked like inviting places to hide, and I tried to think of some plan to get away.

I figured if there were only some way to run away from them, it would be a cinch to hide along the alcoves of those little shops that were closed. We passed along the doorways, and then came out under some stairs. I wasn't sure where the attack came from. I guess whoever did it was standing on the stairway that we walked past.

A hail of fish rained down. One smacked Rick right in the face. Janet and the Walters lady were pelted with them, too. A voice yelled, "Beat it, Scruggs!"

I didn't wait but ran back the way we'd come, through an alleyway with the small stores on one side and the supporting poles of the second floor on the other.

I burst out onto the street and ran back toward Giarhdelli Square. Behind me, I heard somebody else running, too. Whoever it was, he was going fast. There was a horse and carriage waiting at Pier 41. I could feel whoever was behind me getting close enough to tackle me as we raced for that carriage.

"Get going!" I yelled to the driver. "Fast!"

My foot found one of the iron steps on the side, and I leaped. But I slipped. One hand grabbed part of the iron framework, and I hoisted myself up while I heard the driver cluck to the horse.

Just when I felt safe, I heard someone leap right after me and land square in the narrow seat across from me. I jumped to tackle him and fight for it.

## Chapter Fourteen
# A Carriage Ride

"Scruggs, wait!" It was a girl's voice. For a minute I thought it was Janet, but in the dimness I could see long, straight hair.

"Talk fast," I said.

"It's Tom's wife!" she told me.

Meanwhile, the driver was reining in the horse. "Don't stop now," I said. "We gotta get out of here!"

"Please!" Jeannie Blancke exclaimed. "This boy's been kidnaped. Take us to a policeman or somebody."

"Get up!" the driver said, and I realized it was a woman, too. But even in summer the wharf is cold at night, and she had been bundled in a lap robe and a heavy jacket. She turned around as the horse made a steady trot along the street. "No cops along here that I can see," she told us. "But I know a good hiding place closer to Giarhdelli Square."

I turned to Jeannie. "Was that you and Tom up there?" I asked.

"Yes," she was shivering. "Pardon me. My teeth keep chattering. We lugged those fish along from the nearest stand—It was Tom's idea—"

"Here." I pulled off my jacket and gave it to her. "Wear this." She wrapped it around herself and stopped shivering.

"Tom and I agreed that I would follow you while he held them off," she said. "He should be able to get away on the top boardwalk."

"But how did you know where I was?"

"Tom had been watching Walters' headquarters in Palo Alto. He saw you make your escape, but they were swarming out after you with guns, so he couldn't interfere. Then he figured you would go to Mr. Birky. He had met Mr. Birky at the airport, and he traced him to Mountain View. We were going to talk to you there tonight, once we'd heard that the police had been with you. Then Tom thought he saw Walters pass us on East Rengstorff Street. We saw the kidnapping but were pretty helpless. We didn't want to lose sight of you, but we didn't have anything to fight them with ourselves. Tom was afraid they might have come for revenge. So we followed them, and pretty soon Tom was sure they would take you to Pier 39. He's much more informed on their activities than I am, but I think he knew of their plan to pass the laser crystal—"

"*Tom* knows they stole that laser crystal?" I asked. Even the driver turned around on that.

Jeannie nodded. "Yes. You see, Tom's a physicist. He helped design the laser crystal. He's been wild to get it back, and the Federal agents have been keeping him informed and letting him help track it down. They were absolutely sure that the Walters gang had taken it, but they had to catch them *with* the crystal. We had no idea how they would try to pass it off, until you came on the scene."

"I was their stooge," I said. "Is that it?"

"I wouldn't call it that," she told me gently. "They probably planned to plant the crystal on you and then have their contact take it off your person."

Something inside me started seething. "I'm gonna get them for that," I muttered.

Jeannie said nothing. "They took me away from my home," I said between my teeth. "Just when I was learning to be—" I caught myself. I was going to say, "be happy," but I didn't want to spill my guts in front of these two. Suddenly I missed Mrs. Bennett worse than ever, and when I thought about *why* I had been taken away—the real reason—to be the fall guy for a bunch of crooks, I couldn't stand it.

"Scruggs, did you have a happy home in Wisconsin?" Jeannie asked.

"I could have," I told her. "My Sunday-school teacher was going to take me in as her foster son. I guess you think that's pretty funny, huh?"

"No, I don't think that's funny," she said gently. Then I felt like a crumb. I'd been supposing that Jeannie would laugh like Rick and Susan Walters had laughed at me. But it was nice to realize that not everybody had the same outlook as those crooks.

The driver swung the horse down a narrow lane between two crab stands. There was a wharf out back where fishing boats could unload. She swung the carriage between two small rows of parked cars and reined in. Jeannie and I jumped down. "Perfect!" Jeannie said to her. "What do we owe you?"

In the light from the electric candle on the carriage, I saw the driver touch her cap. "Rescue services go for free. What will you two do from here?"

"Find the police," Jeannie said.

"And watch Pier 39," I added. "At least until Tom gets back safely. Where were you supposed to rendezvous with him?" I asked her.

"The courtyard of the Cannery," she said. The Cannery was another set of stores like Ghiardelli Square.

"Why don't you find the police and let me meet Tom?" I asked her. She seemed too wet to spend much longer out of doors. And after a day of jumping through windows and hanging off roofs, I was too tired to push on any more. I didn't feel like running after city buses and telling the police another long story.

Jeannie agreed. "I'll give you a ride to the Cannery," the driver said to me. So I swung up into the carriage. Jeannie disappeared on the other side of the cars, and the driver pulled the carriage forward far enough so that we could watch her get over to Giarhdelli Square and catch a cable car that would at least get her away from the Wharf.

Then we drove out, and the driver said, "My name's Myshell."

"I'm Scruggs," I called to her over the clop-clopping of the horse's hooves.

"Sounds like you've had quite an adventure here."

"Big deal," I told her. "I want to go home to Peabody."

"I can understand why. Maybe if you can find this Tom person, you can call it a day and go back."

"I hope so." We were clop-clopping toward a wide brick gateway, the entrance to the Cannery. Myshell would have reined in, but just then I saw Rick in the shadows, skulking around like he was looking for me.

"Keep going!" I exclaimed in a whisper, and she kept going. Traffic was light at that time of night. I leaned forward and said in a low voice, "I'm going to jump off on the street side of the carriage and run for the stands over there."

"Did you see one of those thieves waiting for you?" she asked.

"Either waiting for me or just looking for me. I don't want to risk going in."

She gave a brief nod, and then hurriedly pulled out a business card and handed it to me. "I'll be back at eight in the morning. You know how to find me if you need help."

"Thanks."

She kept the horse going at a steady but slow pace. My foot found the step, and I leaped off, and then ran for the shelter of some closed-down crab stands.

## Chapter Fifteen

# Finding the Juggler

I woke up before dawn—starving.

Even then, Fisherman's Wharf wasn't quiet. Boats along the piers were putting out into the bay to fish. I could hear them chugging sluggishly to life, and the men were calling back and forth. Sea gulls were crying. It seemed so pretty, so peaceful, for a minute. But then I thought of Tom and remembered the danger he must be in.

Seemed obvious to me that they had caught him. Maybe, I told myself, the police would rescue him. From what it sounded like, the net was closing in on the Walters gang—more than Susan Walters even suspected.

But then I shook the thought away. Every minute was precious as far as Tom was concerned. It wouldn't take the crooks long to figure out that they were better off with him twenty feet under water.

I crept out of my place behind a row of trash cans along the crab stand. Dawn was rising. The fishing boats had put out and were dotting the waters past Alcatraz Island out in the bay.

I stumbled along, trying to wake up and looking down at the empty harbor. Not many boats were left—a couple of tour craft for Alcatraz or the bay and a few disabled fishing boats. One bigger, nicer boat was bobbing with the rest. I can't say what drew my attention to it, maybe the three circles on its prow. One was blue, one red, and one green. They reminded me of juggling. Then the swell shifted, and the name on the hull was partly visible—Jug—

*The Juggler!*

I whipped down to the harbor and took a better look. It seemed dead and still, nobody on board. I slipped my shoes and socks off, slid down into the still water, and struck out for it.

First I swam around it, every now and then looking around to make sure that nobody was watching the harbor. Then at last I found the ladder and swung up onto it.

I came up cautiously over the side. Still no reaction.

After I listened for a long time, I found the door to the cabins and went below. I searched through a couple of cramped rooms, walked into another, and almost fell over a body on the floor. But it was a warm and breathing body, half-hidden under a blanket. I snatched the cover back.

"Tom!" I whispered urgently. "Tom!" He was sleeping deeply. There was an angry red weal under one eye, and the left side of his lower lip was swollen. I pulled and tugged him clear of the blanket. Somebody had tied him up—probably Rick, judging from the hard knots.

I went out into the narrow galley and found a knife. Then I came back and cut the ropes, all the time calling to him.

There was a thermos of cold coffee lying in another cabin. I threw the coffee into his face, and at last he stirred.

"Get up! Get up!" I whispered fiercely. "We're both gonna be shark bait if you don't wake up!"

He started to come around, and let me haul him to the steps. It took a long time to get him up on the deck, even though there were only seven steps to climb. But once the salt air hit him, he revived some more.

"Can't walk right," he mumbled to me. He seemed to know it was me and that I was trying to help him escape.

"Can you swim?" I asked him.

"Can you—tow me in there?"

That was a thought. There were round life preservers—mostly for decoration, I guess—hanging on a rope on the bulkhead. I got one and threw it overboard. "Come on, try to jump," I told him. "Easy does it. That's the way."

He half-jumped and half-fell overboard, and I dived after him. The water braced him up some. I got the large life preserver around him, and it kept him afloat while I pulled for the walkway. At last we were holding solid wood.

"Man, what did they give you to knock you out?" I asked him.

I helped him climb up. "I don't know," he whispered. "We've got to get out of here."

I helped him up the steps and grabbed my socks and shoes. Then we made our way along the street. People were opening up their stores and stalls, and a lot of them stared at us.

"Chinatown," he mumbled. "The cable cars."

I sat him on a bench at the trolley park and got tickets. More people were milling around. It was a little past eight. I sat down beside Tom and put on my socks and shoes. It took a long time to get a cable car up to Chinatown. That's almost the only place the cable cars go anymore. Now San Francisco uses buses for its real transportation, although the buses run on the cables too.

Seemed like we'd never get one. It was getting late. I had spent a long time struggling with Tom. His waterproof watch read 9:30. Wherever the Walters gang had hurried off to, they would surely be noticing the time and hurrying back to their boat again before the cops traced Tom or put two and two together and searched the only boats left in the harbor. Maybe, I told myself, they would never spot us in the crowd of people waiting for a cable car ride.

At last we got on a car and headed up the steep hill from the Wharf. I held onto a pole and kept my other arm gripped around Tom's arm, steadying him as he hung on for the ride.

The buildings became narrower and more crowded together. The hills steepened, and we swung up into Chinatown. I must have been bug-eyed at the sight. Storefronts were printed in Chinese with English subtitles. The smell of fish drifted across the street—remains of last night's catch. Though crammed together on the steep hills, some of the buildings were five or six stories tall, with elaborate fronts made to look like golden pagodas.

At first it looked downright elegant. But Tom nudged me to get off, and when the car slowed on the crest of a hill, we leaped off, and I helped him to the curb. The sidewalk was already filling with tourists and Chinese residents.

"Not the nice section," he said weakly. "Farther up. Come on."

I helped him climb the steep hill as we went up. The storefronts looked more and more fake and worn. The smells were stronger. Tom pointed me to a narrow doorway crammed between a kind of deli and a souvenir place. In the window of the Chinese deli hung two roast suckling pigs and three roast chickens. The chickens had their heads on.

I gulped and pushed through the narrow doorway. We went up a narrow flight of steps and found ourselves in a worn-looking lobby. The place was a hotel. I never found out the name because the writing on the door was in Chinese.

I left Tom on a chair and ordered a room.

"My buddy there is sick," I told the clerk. He looked at Tom and and me and frowned. After all, we were soaking wet, but Tom pulled a MasterCard out of his wallet, and the clerk let me register. I signed us in by our real names. I figured that Walters would have to do a lot of searching before she found this hotel, and if Tom's wife knew about this place, I wanted her to find us.

I helped Tom up the narrow stairs again, and a bellboy led us to a room with two beds. It was more like a real bedroom than a hotel room—nothing fancy, but perfectly clean and made up, with a Gideon Bible on the nightstand.

Tom fell onto one of the beds. I didn't think it was healthy for him to fall asleep soaking wet. I pulled off his shoes, socks, and jacket and got the rest of him under the covers. I was still starving, but I wouldn't leave him yet.

I stood at the window, and then went back to the Bible and touched it. I wondered what Jack and Penny and Mrs. Bennett were doing right then.

Sure enough, Mrs. Bennett had gotten my first letter, but Walters had intercepted her reply and had substituted a fake. Then Walters had gotten a sample of my handwriting so that they could send Mrs. Bennett a fake answer. What would it be? A letter telling her to get out of my life, or telling her that I'd given up on Christianity? They would think of something efficient and cruel to say and then try to make it sound like me. I rummaged through a ramshackle desk in the room and found paper. I sat down to write to her. But for a long time I sat staring at the paper. A guy as dumb as me doesn't write well, so first I played everything through my mind and figured out what I would tell her and how I would say it. I must have sat there a good hour. Then I realized the time was going, so I began to write.

Dear Mother,

Then I hesitated. If I told Mrs. Bennett all about Susan Walters and all the fights I'd been in, it would just worry her. She was probably worried already.

Please don't worry. I'm okay. My aunt turned out to be a crook who wanted to make me a crook because I don't have any relatives who would have cared. She didn't know how much I wanted to come and be your son. They intercepted one of your letters to me. They might send you a fake letter from me.

I'm staying in Chinatown with a friend. I will be home soon. I love you very much.

Scruggs

Something warm was on my face, and I brushed it away.

"Soon enough I'll get back there," I told myself sternly. "No need for boo-hooing about it now."

My voice made Tom stir. He looked at me. "Go on, get some pork buns, okay?" he said. "Coffee, too." He pulled his wallet out and tossed it to me. "I'll get up soon. I feel better."

I took the key and went out into the narrow hallway with the threadbare carpet. I was glad Tom had given me an errand, because I didn't want to sit and cry like a baby.

But I felt humble, and I prayed a quick prayer. *Please protect me from them—and from myself. Please take me home to Wisconsin, Lord.* I had no idea how quickly He was going to answer the first half of the prayer.

## Chapter Sixteen
# Chinatown

The street smelled sort of steamy, like the first clouds of cooking were coming out from doors opening and closing. My stomach got tied in a knot with hunger. But one look at those whole chickens hanging in the window next door cured me enough to keep looking.

I was just walking along, watching everything in those narrow, steep streets, keeping up with the slogging crowd, when all of a sudden, a Chinese girl comes popping out of a parking alley.

"Please, oh please, won't you help me? My brother! My brother! Please help!"

At first she just kind of came out and said it—real loud and urgent—to anybody listening. But when she saw me looking at her, she grabbed my arm. "Please stop them! They'll hurt him!"

So I ducked into the alley after her without thinking that I was in a tough part of Chinatown and had all the looks of a tourist. Just past some cars, there were two kids in black vinyl jackets holding a little kid up off the ground. He was kicking and screaming. One of the bigger kids had a hold of him, and the other one was cuffing his head and face.

It made my blood boil, and I tapped the second one on the shoulder. "Say, Buddy—" and when he turned around, I popped him a light punch to his chest just to tell him to get moving or else. Then the girl screamed, because the other one was about to clobber me from behind, but as soon as he let go of the little kid, the little kid tore into him—screaming, yelling, biting, crying—the works.

The guy I had tapped ran off, and the other one—once he got loose—ran off too.

"Say, it's okay, Buster," I started to say to the little guy. But then he jumped at me, yowling and fighting. "Hey kid! I'm on your side!" I yelled.

"You let them get away!" he screamed. "You dirty rotten bum! They took her money!" All this time he was hitting me. I didn't want to do it, but I picked him up and pinned him to the wall until he calmed down. "Let 'em get away?" I asked him. "They were giving you the tar-and-feather treatment!"

"I don't care! I'd have killed them! And I'll kill you!" he screamed, flailing at me and crying. Between avoiding his kicks, I looked at her. She looked helpless and embarrassed.

"They stole my purse," she said, in perfect English with no accent. But then she spoke to him in Chinese. I think she was telling him to calm down. It didn't do any good.

At first I thought the kid might need a slap across the face to bring him out of it. But then I figured, no, it looked to me like he'd been hit enough all his life. That was what had put him into his rage—being hit by those purse-snatchers.

Then suddenly it was like the very thing I thought about him got turned around in my mind, and it was being said about me. Like all of a sudden I had found my own problem.

I looked down at him, still crying and fighting, and I saw myself, Scruggs the window-buster, the guy who flew into rages that no one could stop. This kid was a nine- or ten-year-old Chinese kid from the West Coast, and I was a teenage white kid from Wisconsin, but we were the same. Except, somewhere in my life, a Person had picked me up and was waiting—without slapping me around—to make me quit struggling.

I think when the kid felt me staring at him that way— surprised and sorry and sort of stunned, he started to quiet down. "It was all we had," he whimpered. Then he really started to cry, and I let him down, and he ran to his older sister.

"Look," I said to her. "I have some money—"

"No," she said quickly. "No, we don't take charity. We just wanted to go out. The money wasn't that important. We'll go home and have lunch."

Now that I'd helped her, she was eager to get away— embarrassed by him and by all that had happened. And, like a dummy, I just stood there and let them walk away, even though there were a hundred things I wanted to tell them. Like how that kid and me were alike, and how the Lord had saved me.

But they didn't want to hear it, and I let them go.

I walked out of the alley and found a bakery. I didn't know what was what under the counter. But I asked for pork rolls—a half dozen, and then I bought coffee in styrofoam cups with lids. The man who waited on me was friendly, and his baked stuff looked fresh and hot, but I felt like I stuck out, being so big and gangly among all those small, trim people sitting in the bakery.

The streets were crowding up some more, filling with tourists looking for places to have lunch. I found my way back to the hotel without any more adventures.

When I got back up to our room, Tom was awake and looking better.

"Did you get lost?" he asked me.

"No, I—uh—met some kids," I told him.

"You get into a fight?"

"Kind of got into the middle of one," I said. But he saw I didn't want to talk about it, so he let it drop.

"I called Jeannie," he told me between mouthfuls of pork bun. "She got sidetracked by the police. But she's going to run down here real fast and take you back to Mountain View. Your uncle can get you on another plane and get you home."

"What about you?" I asked.

"I'm staying right here. I've got to get that crystal back, and I feel better being close to the Wharf. This gang likes to operate in crowded places. Chinatown and the Wharf area seem likely."

"Then I'm staying, too," I told him. "I'll help you find that crystal. I figure you and Jeannie need me to even up the sides in this game. You know, three of us against three of them."

"It's a pretty dangerous game we're playing."

"That's okay."

"I thought you wanted to go home."

"I do, but I'm not going to run out on you now. You and Jeannie took a big risk to get me out of trouble last night. I owe it to you, and I want to help out." I bit into another pork bun. "By the way," I said with my mouth full, "why was that gang so dumb as to leave you alone aboard *The Juggler?*"

"That's the odd thing," he told me. "They were dead certain late last night that you were back in Mountain

View. Walters and the other two were working on something in the next room, and I heard them talking. They went out to get you, thinking you were at Mr. Birky's, and let me tell you, they went loaded down with enough firearms to hold off a platoon of marines. Then along about four in the morning, they came back all mad, and that's when Rick gave me a shot of whatever it was that knocked me out. But just as I was going out, I heard them saying you were in Los Altos—that's up by Stanford, exactly where I live. After that they must have gone up there to get you and missed you again. In the meantime, you found me."

He frowned. "I'm just glad Jeannie's all right. For all I know, they may have driven right past our house—well, except she wasn't there much. Over the phone just now she told me she'd spent a good part of the night with the police and your aunt and uncle. Then she went home and washed and changed and went to the police station to make a positive ID of Rick and Janet. Nobody seems to know where those two popped in from." He crammed another half of a roll into his mouth. "Anyway, when I couldn't reach her by phone at home, I got your uncle's number and called him, and he told me where she was, so I called her at the station—"

Just then there was a knock at the door. "I think that's her," he said.

It was. She came in with a paper bag. "Here's your jacket back," she said pleasantly, as though she'd taken it to have it pressed and nothing else was going on. "Hi, honey," she said, giving Tom a kiss and then wrinkling up her nose. "Smells like pork buns. Is that what you're living on?"

"For now," he told her. "What's up? Anything new?"

"Not much. No success with the mug shots, even though I pored over them all night—all morning, anyway," she said. "I was there from about 5:00 A.M. until 10:00. They thought if we could identify everyone in the gang we might be able to identify or figure out the contact."

Tom sighed, defeated for the moment.

"Funny thing," she added. "The police thought they spotted Walters and her crew up in Los Altos and Stanford. Isn't that odd?"

"They thought Scruggs was up there," Tom told her, "Although where they got that crazy notion, I don't know. They want you back, Scruggs. Why? Do you know something? Surely they would realize that by now you've spilled all the beans anyway."

I shrugged. "I'm pretty dumb, Tom," I told him. "Last night I was just supposed to walk into that video arcade and play out my roll of quarters. That's all. I don't know how that would have helped them. But they told me I better do it." I reached into the pocket of the jacket. "Here's the quarters. Do you think something might be attached to one of them?"

Tom opened the roll and glanced at them. "That would be a clumsy way of doing it, certainly," he said. "No, these are fine. The crystal would be way too big to stick to a quarter and have it fit into an arcade slot, and there's no microfilm hidden here."

Jeannie frowned. "Maybe they just wanted you occupied," she said. "Maybe somebody else was supposed to do all the work in getting the laser crystal from you." She knelt down and looked at the hem of my pants. "Nothing."

I laughed at her, looking in the hem like that for the crystal. "I may be dumb, but I'd notice some guy trying to pull a laser crystal out of the cuff of my jeans," I told her.

Tom nodded. "But she's right. You said they gave you these clothes and the jacket. That would explain why they've taken so many risks to capture you again—leaving me on *The Juggler* and driving around together were terribly dangerous for them. But they had to risk it—you've got the laser crystal on you somewhere!"

"It would have been easiest to have taken it from the jacket," Jeannie said quickly. Tom hurriedly laid it inside out on the bed and felt the seams along the lining. "Jeannie!" he cried. "It is! It's here! Safe with us!" The guy's eyes were actually wet. That thing was his baby.

He ripped part of the lining with his penknife and pulled out a sealed plastic package. "We've got it! We've got it! They would have sent him into the arcade, and their contact would have come and taken the crystal while Scruggs was playing a video game. It was nothing an experienced pickpocket couldn't have done!" He grinned at her triumphantly.

"What now?" I asked.

"Whatever you want," he told me. "The case is solved, and we've got the crystal. You can have a vacation with us or go back to Peabody, Scruggs."

"I'd like to visit you for sure," I told him, "But—"

"I know, I know—you really want to go home. Okay. Let's go call the police. Better yet, let's drop this off, and then go celebrate."

First I put the jacket on, because I wanted to keep it as a souvenir. We started for the phone in the hall, but then I said, "Wait a second, I want to write to somebody real fast." They went out, and I sat down and hurriedly added a line to the letter to Mrs. Bennett:

P.S. I just helped my two friends get a little gizmo that got stolen from them. I will be coming home very soon, and I will tell you the rest. Everything is all right now.

I wanted to add a line about what happened in the alley, but I didn't know how to explain it, so I let it go.

Out in the hall, Tom and Jeannie were still on the phone. Jeannie looked at me, wanting me to join in with their happiness.

"I'd like to mail this," I told her. "But there are no envelopes or stamps around."

"I think if you ask the man at the desk, he can get you some, maybe even mail the letter," she told me while Tom talked on the phone to one of the other men who had developed the crystal.

I ran downstairs and asked the clerk, and he smiled and said he could do that for me, so I paid him for the stamp and addressed the letter. Then the clerk looked past me and said, "Can I help you, sir?"

I don't even know why I did it—maybe I just guessed the truth. But I glanced behind me, and there was Rick. Right behind me.

## Chapter Seventeen
# The Last Battle

His big hands dropped onto my shoulders. I moved without thinking. My two hands grabbed the heavy ledger and swung it into the side of his face with the biggest wallop you ever saw.

He let go, and I shoulder-butted him away, then ran for the door. Wouldn't you know it—Walters was there with Janet, blocking the way. I yelled fierce and wild like I'd mow 'em down, and Janet ducked.

I still had the ledger in my hands, and without thinking I shoved it at Susan Walters. Automatically, her hands closed on it, and I used it to push her out of the way as I went through the door behind them.

Then I was running like a sprinter up that steep hill. I could outdistance the women, but I knew Rick would be on top of me before I knew it.

The sidewalks were getting too crowded for good running. A couple of times, I almost fell. So, even though it made me more visible, I ran in the street and tried to avoid the cars.

But I could hear him pushing people as they yelped or exclaimed. He was still gaining. I ducked into an alley.

Overhead there was a fire escape—one of those steel stairways outside of old buildings. But the bottom was folded up like a ladder. I jumped, grabbed a rung of the grating on the landing, and somehow or another swung myself up onto it. Then I was climbing and climbing, clattering up those steps and praying it would take me to the roof. Every now and then from higher and higher up, I would look through the grating rungs. No Rick yet.

I made it to the roof and looked down—seven dizzy flights. There he was, just stumbling into the alley, looking left and right for me. He looked puzzled. I hoped he'd figure he'd taken the wrong turn.

I would have thought I had lost him when I'd turned into the alley and then climbed the fire escape. At least, I told myself, he wasn't smart enough to think of the fire escape, even though he'd figured I'd taken the alley.

Then he seemed to be looking around, turning really slowly. I dropped onto my stomach and watched through the fire escape, using it as a cover.

Then I saw him with something black in his hand—a gun I figured—and suddenly he looked up at the fire escape and grinned. In another instant he swung up and was coming after me.

I ran across the roof. There was another roof close by—one short jump away. It was either jump or face Rick. I jumped for it, landed with a thud on the next roof, and darted down the fire escape.

By my reasoning, Rick would give up when he came up on the roof and didn't see me. He would know he had lost me. I waited around to make sure, hiding behind a trash can down below in an alley between the two buildings. Our little game had turned to hide-and-seek, but I was sure I could win it.

Rick came to the edge of the first roof above me, and again he seemed to me to be casting around like a dog on my trail. Then he leaped over, too, and came down the fire escape.

I ran for it again, through the crowded sidewalk, taking this street and that street, twisting my ankle on the steep hill. I came around the corner and almost stumbled into Susan Walters! We both screamed. A cable car was going by, and I made one terrific leap, pushed my way through it, and jumped out the other side.

Then I sprinted again, but my lungs were burning and my ankle smarted with each step. They were closing in on me—even Rick, who wasn't very bright.

They think I've still got the crystal, I told myself. That's what they want. They must be sure I've got it because they aren't chasing Tom and Jeannie, just me.

Even while I was pounding along, my mind was replaying the sight of Rick casting around for me. How had he known exactly where to find me? It was like he was tracking me by scent or something. They were all tracking me, trying to close in on different sides.

Far away, a siren blared. Was that for me? I wondered. Were the cops going to come and save me in time?

Not very easily, they weren't. There was Walters at the next corner with what looked like a gun in her hand. I went down an alley. The police were never going to find me before the Walters gang cornered me. They had my trail.

Then somehow I suddenly got it. They really were tracking me. They knew my exact location, and they were sure of it, just as sure as they'd been last night when they'd gone all the way up to Los Altos.

No, I hadn't been in Los Altos last night, but my jacket had been. They'd been following my jacket—first going to Mountain View when Jeannie had taken it with her on her stop at the Birkys', then to *The Juggler* when they'd lost its range, to track it from a powerful tracking device aboard their boat, then to Stanford when Jeannie had gone home to wash, and then to Los Altos. They hadn't been able to do anything when they'd finally caught up to her in Los Altos, because she'd been with the police, and they had been looking for me anyway, not knowing the jacket was in her bag. So when she walked out, they'd let her go, not bothering to check their smaller tracking gear until she was on her way down here—and even then they hadn't figured it out.

And, I realized, that was why they were sure I had the crystal. It was obvious if I hadn't found the radio transmitter in the jacket, I hadn't found the crystal, either. I am dumb, but they thought I was even dumber.

At first I was ready to ditch the jacket, but then I decided I might as well make use of it. I ducked around a corner and waited. In another minute, I heard Rick running up. I pulled off the jacket, and as he came around the corner, I flung it over his head so that he couldn't see.

I got a glimpse of that black thing in his hand. It wasn't a gun but a little black box with a long, thin antenna— a tracking device.

Then I shoved him like all I wanted to do was get away. He clawed at the jacket, and I ran off again, ducking into a souvenir shop. There was a huge circular rack of robes and kimonos in there, and I dived right into them, then hunkered down and peeked out.

I could see the sidewalk through the glass windows of the store. Rick went racing by, looking like he had just struck gold. He had the jacket clutched in his hands and was trying to find Susan Walters or Janet, eager to show them that he'd recaptured the jacket. It must not have occurred to him to check for the crystal.

Then a police car slid by, lights flashing. I leaped out from the kimonos—a customer screamed when I popped

out—and raced for the door, hoping the cops would see me and pick me up. Another police car followed the first one down the steep hill, while goggle-eyed tourists and Chinese shopkeepers came out and stared.

I flagged down the second police car. Tom Blancke was on the passenger side.

I ran around to his side and jumped in. "Get us back to the hotel!" I yelled to the policeman. "Rick thinks he has the laser crystal! He'll head for their car. It must be parked close to the hotel where they cornered me!"

I don't know how much the policeman understood of that, but he did what I asked him.

"And make sure that boat is covered, too," Tom said. "They might try to get to it if they think we've got them trapped up here."

The cop talked into his radio, and suddenly switched the siren on. He swung around a steep corner and followed Tom's directions back to the hotel.

"At least we'll get Rick," Tom said. "We spotted him."

"You should get all three," I told him. "They had the jacket bugged with a transmitter. They've been following it all night, trying to get the crystal back. Now that Rick's got it, they'll follow him."

The radio was going a mile a minute, but cops talk in numbers, and I couldn't follow what the dispatcher was saying. Tom understood it, though.

"They'll have plainclothes men at the hotel," he told me. "We'll get them this time!"

We swung up another street that led up to the hotel.

"There it is!" I yelled, pointing at the car I had been driven in the night before. It was pulling out.

"Don't worry," the policeman at the wheel said. "They aren't going anywhere."

On the steepest part of the hill, two police cars slid out from a crossroads and cut them off. An unmarked car behind them suddenly slid up sideways behind them.

I hadn't seen a single policeman in San Francisco before that day, and all of a sudden the street was full of them— all in cars, too. They hemmed the Walters crew in like a logjam on all sides.

I felt Tom's huge hand gripping my shoulder. "We got them! We got them, Scruggs!"

# Chapter Eighteen
# Going Home

I kept my eyes shut on the ascent. It still made my heart go into my throat to see the plane tipped up like that. But during the time I was so scared, I let my mind play back the last day and a half.

Tom and Jeannie had made me a dinner that would have done honor to a king. They both enjoyed gourmet cooking. I'd met their cat, Bear, who was only half manx. Full-blooded manxes have no tails, but since Bear was only half, he had a little bunny tail. Tom had helped me perfect my juggling, and they had put me up for the night.

My suitcases were stuffed with chocolates from Ghiardelli Square for Mrs. Bennett. Tom and Jeannie and I had taken a quick spin back to the Square after dinner. I'd run right up to Stevie's Sweeties while they looked around, and the lady—Mrs. Sugar—had remembered me from when I'd been there with Rick.

She hadn't seen the evening papers and didn't know all about the laser crystal caper, and for some reason, I hadn't told her. I'd just told her I was going back home to my mother in Peabody, Wisconsin, and I wanted to take her some chocolates.

Then she'd filled me up with free samples, I think because she was happy I wasn't hanging around with bad company anymore.

We'd looked and looked for Myshell the carriage driver. Tom had taken Jeannie and me for a carriage ride, but Myshell must have had the night off. Our driver promised to tell Myshell I was all right and on my way home.

At last the plane was leveling off. I opened one eye and looked past the two people sitting next to me. Down below were craggy mountains, black and white at this distance.

I had a couple sitting next to me—Susan and Rollin. They were engaged to be married, and even though they weren't as lively as the McCunes had been, I was glad I sat next to them.

For one thing, I'd been around Rick and Susan Walters so long, I'd almost forgotten that people could care about anything other than money. So I was glad when Susan told me that Rollin was working his way through college, and she had a job in San Diego. They liked working, and they liked each other, and I was glad, because I knew Rick had been wrong when he'd told me money was everything.

Rollin could tell I was scared of flying, so he talked to me about soccer. He was from Peru—an exchange student—and he'd grown up playing soccer. He took my mind off the way the plane was jolting around over the Rockies.

After a little less than an hour, we were back over the wide open spaces, and I let myself doze, thinking about everything that had happened.

Just that very morning, while the Blanckes had been taking me to the airport, I'd given them my testimony. I was surprised when they didn't laugh at me. (That was from living too close to Rick again.) I'd told them about how I used to break windows and fly into rages, and how when I'd seen that little kid in Chinatown, God had put a new understanding into my heart. Tom had only said, "I hope that God helps you understand that you aren't really dumb either, Scruggs."

That had stopped me for a minute. I've always been dumb. Jeannie had seemed to read my mind.

"Anybody who can think on his feet like you isn't dumb. You're a smart kid. If you really believe in God as much as you say, then you ought to give Him credit for what He's done."

Maybe, I told myself as I felt the plane skim along, I'm not as dumb as I thought I was. At least I'll start studying in school again. I can always try.

Like Jeannie had said, if the Lord had given me brains, I ought to give Him the credit instead of denying it.

But it was a new and uncomfortable thought. Sometimes it's sort of comfortable to think you're dumb. Still, I wanted to be a good testimony, especially to Tom and Jeannie, now that we were friends.

That was another new thing. At the airport, they had hugged me good-bye. Jeannie had kissed my cheek, and Tom had shaken hands with me, and already they were planning for me to join them for a week over next Christmas vacation. Mr. and Mrs. Birky were there to see me off too.

"Too bad you can't stay around here a few more days. Jack and Penny will be flying out for a visit," Mr. Birky said.

But I told him I was ready to get back home. He just nodded his head.

Mrs. Birky squeezed my hand and whispered, "Come back to see us soon, Little Bill."

It was strange to think I'd gone out there all by myself and made friends—real friends. They hadn't felt sorry for me at all, and they hadn't felt obliged to me; they just liked me. That was new to me.

By that time Rollin was awake, and I told him about it. He woke up Susan and told her I was the kid from the newspapers last night. Then they both got excited and wanted to hear all about everything.

Of course the newspapers had blown everything up the wrong way, making a big deal out of how I'd gotten Tom off *The Juggler* by myself and what an important person he was to have helped develop the laser crystal. That seemed to make the reporters think it was an even bigger deal for me to have rescued him.

But the big deal to me was how Tom had been trying to help me all along and had been so ready to get me away from the Walters gang. And I'd rescued Tom because he was Tom, not because of anything else. Tom doesn't even *look* like a scientist as far as I'm concerned. He seems too easygoing and nice to be important.

Then Rollin and Susan wanted to know who had left that note on my door a month ago, and I told them we had figured it to be Janet. She had been assigned to follow me around in Peabody and keep an eye on things from that end. She must have been fighting with her conscience the whole time, and I guess that note was her way of giving in to it one last time before she threw her lot in with Walters.

Poor Janet. I felt sorry for her more than the others. She'd always been nice to me, anyway.

At last the plane began to circle, and I was too excited to be scared. We came down smoothly, taxied to the gate at the terminal, and at last the stewardess said we could go.

The aisle filled up, and the whole time my heart was pounding hard, and I had a lump in my throat. I could feel that my face was all red, like it usually gets. At last the line of people was moving, up the aisle, then up the covered ramp, then out into the terminal, and I looked around wildly, just like the first time I'd been there.

Then I saw her, and I knew the adventure was over and done with, forever. I was back home, and it would always be here, no matter where I went or how long I stayed away.

A guy who's a Christian and a foster kid holds onto things in his mind, storing them up. Now I go to a Christian school and wear a tight tie every day except Saturdays. I play basketball like other guys, and every night I eat home cooking like other guys. But sometimes when Mother (that's what I call her now) is setting the table or doing cross-stitch in her favorite chair, I watch her and store away the picture in my mind.